KB085209

슬로우 불릿

도서출판 아시아에서는 《바이링궐 에디션 한국 현대 소설》을 기획하여 한국의 우수한 문학을 주제별로 엄선해 국내외 독자들에게 소개합니다. 이 기획은 국내외 우수한 번역가들이 참여하여 원작의 품격을 최대한 살렸습니다. 문학을 통해 아시아의 정체성과 가치를 살피는 데 주력해 온 도서출판 아시아는 한국인의 삶을 넓고 깊게 이해하는 데 이 기획이 기여하기를 기대합니다.

Asia Publishers present some of the very best modern Korean litera-ture to readers worldwide through its new Korean literature series 〈Bi-lingual Edition Modern Korean Literature〉. We are proud and happy to offer it in the most authoritative translation by renowned translators of Korean literature. We hope that this series helps to build solid bridges between citizens of the world and Koreans through rich in-depth understanding of Korea.

바이링궐 에디션 한국 현대 소설 017

Bi-lingual Edition Modern Korean Literature 017

Slow Bullet

이대환

슬로우 불릿

Lee Dae-hwan

ASIA
PUBLISHERS

Contents

슬로우 불릿

Slow Bullet

인간이 슬픔을 알게 하는 그 영혼의 신비만은 영원히 생명과학에게 들키지 않기를 소망하는 나는 이 소설을 바친다. 고통의 유령과 같은 베트남전쟁 고엽제 후유증에 시달리는 세계의 모든 이와 그의 가족, 그리고 스스로 죽음을 극복하여 인간의 야수적 교만을 푸르게 비웃어주는 베트남 대지의 위대한 초목에게.

*

아직 어둑새벽은 멀었다. 호미곶 앞바다가 수런수런 깨어나며 물결을 일으킨다. 하늘에는 별들이 된바람을 맞은 호롱불처럼 가뭇없이 지워지고 있다. 짙은 구름이 뭍으로 번져오는 모양이다. 하지만 갯마을은 아늑히 잠들었다.

I hope life science never solves the mystery of our soul, its ability to feel sorrow. I dedicate this story to all the victims suffering from those phantoms of pain, the aftereffects of defoliants used in the Vietnam War, to their families, and to the great greenery of the Vietnamese land, which mocks the savagery of human arrogance through its triumph over death.

*

It was still a while until daybreak. On the sea, waking up and murmuring off Cape Homi, the rip-

9

한반도의 전도(全圖)를 호랑이 형상에 비유한 풍수지리 달인이 영물의 꼬리에 해당되는 명당으로 찍었다는 호미곶, 그 호랑이 꼬리의 땅 조각은 보리 냄새를 자욱한 안개처럼 덮어쓴 채 그저 캄캄하고 적막할 따름이다. 단지 호랑이 꼬리의 터럭 하나가 꼼지락거린 것이라 할까. 문득 익수가 눈을 떴다.

그는 오줌이 마려웠으나 침착하게 머리부터 굴렸다. 홑이불을 살그머니 들어올리고, 가만가만 요에서 벗어나고, 소리 없이 방을 빠져나가고, 볼일은 대문 밖에 나가서 본다. 마치 전쟁터의 신병이 엄격한 수칙을 되새기듯 움직일 차례를 또박또박 결정해 나갔다. 아내의 단잠을 건드리지 말아야 한다는 남편의 집착이 순식간에 송곳처럼 뾰족해졌다. 모로 누워서 두 다리를 잔뜩 오그린 숙희는 깊이 잠든 것 같았다.

방문이 훤히 열려 있었다. 이부자리를 깔 때 해놓은 그대로였다. 익수는 그것을 고맙게 여겼다. 문지방 앞의 쪽마루에는 사기요강이 은은한 빛의 덩어리처럼 웅크리고 있었다. 그가 잠깐 무릎을 쓰다듬었다. 뻑뻑한 관절이 문제였다. 제발 뿌드득거리지 마라. 왼손을 무릎에 올리고 오른손으로 바닥을 짚은 그는 거의 빌고 있었다. 요행히

ples were getting bigger. Stars were vanishing in the sky without a trace like flames in small kerosene lamps caught in a gale. Thick clouds were spreading across the land. Yet the fishing village was still snugly asleep. A geomancer supposedly pointed to Cape Homi as one of the most propitious sites in the Korean peninsula, the tail of a metaphorical tiger. This small piece of land was dark and desolate, an aroma of barley rising from it like a dense fog. Stirring like a single hair of the tiger's tail, Ik-su suddenly opened his eyes.

Feeling the urge to urinate, he began calmly thinking about the steps he had to take: First, gently take down the thin blanket, then quietly get off the futon, sneak out of the room noiselessly, and take care of business outside the gate. Like a new conscript trying to remember instructions on the battlefield, he calmly went over each step in his mind. Obsessed with not disturbing his sleeping wife, he became edgy as an awl. Curled up sideways, Suk-hui looked sound asleep.

Ik-su found the door of the room wide open just as they had left it when they spread their futon in the evening. Ik-su felt grateful for that. A porcelain chamber pot crouched like a mass of faint light on

관절이 주인의 뜻을 받들었다.

익수는 쪽마루에 걸터앉아 슬리퍼를 꿰차고 도둑처럼 걸음을 옮겼다. 러닝셔츠와 사각팬티가 너무 헐렁해서 허수아비가 어설프게 걸어가는 꼴이었다. 언제나 활짝 열어두는 대문을 벗어난 그는 자기 집 담벼락에 붙어 섰다. 긴장이 풀렸다. 한숨을 들이마셨다. 어둔 허공에 푸짐히 배인 보리 냄새가 가슴으로 몰려들었다. 그것이 그는 좋았다. 죽음의 냄새가 이런 것인지 모른다는 생각이 또다시 살아났다. 그래서 더 좋았다. 그는 오줌 마려운 것을 깜박 잊어먹은 아이가 즐거이 딴전을 부리듯 자꾸만 한숨을 들이쉬고 있었다.

익수네 집 뒤에 목장처럼 펼쳐진 너른 언덕은 온통 보리밭이다. 봄이 물러나고 그 너머 솔숲에서 뻐꾸기가 울기 시작할 즈음에 보리밭은 마치 망망한 쪽빛 바다 앞에서 굉장한 향연을 준비하듯 찬란한 황금빛으로 변신한다. 해마다 보름 남짓한 그 기간에 익수는 혼자서 집 뒤로 나가 보리밭을 바라보곤 했다. 그런데 올해는 이상했다. 누런 보리밭이 뿜어내는 냄새에서 누룽지를 왕창 집어넣고 푹 끓여낸 숭늉 냄새를 맡았다. 구수한 맛은 본디 누런 빛깔인가 싶고, 자신의 마음에 구수한 맛의 누런 빛깔이 물

the narrow veranda in front of the threshold. He quickly rubbed his knees. His stiff joints were a problem. *Please don't creak*, he was almost praying, with his left hand on his knee and his right hand on the floor. Luckily, his joints obeyed.

Ik-su sat on the narrow veranda, pushed his feet into his slippers, and began moving quietly away like a thief. His undershirt and shorts hung from his body so loosely that he looked like a scarecrow walking awkwardly. Outside the gate his family always left open Ik-su stood right in front of the fence, facing it. He felt relieved. He took a deep breath. The smell of barley permeating the dark air was rushing into his chest. He liked it. He thought again that death might smell like this, and this made him like the aroma even more. He kept taking a deep breath like a distracted child, briefly forgetting that he was about to pee.

The spacious hill behind Ik-su's house, unfolding like a pasture, was entirely covered with barley. Around the time the spring was waning and cuckoos began crying in the pine forest beyond, the barley field turned an intense golden color with the vast indigo sea in the background, as if preparing for a feast. Every year, during this roughly fortnight-

드는 듯했다. 죽음이 삶의 짝이라니 죽음의 세계에도 구수한 보리 냄새가 그득할 것이라는 안도감이 일기도 했다. 그것이 야릇한 소망을 불러올 때도 있었다. 보리밭 저위쪽 가장자리의 외로운 무덤—아련히 멀어진 이십 대 청춘의 어느 희붐한 달빛 아래서 숙희와 잊지 못할 추억을 만들었던 그 자리에 드러누워 아무도 몰래 마지막 숨을 거둘 수만 있다면, 자신은 종점에 닿아서 무엇보다 소중한 행복 하나를 거머쥔 인생이 될 것 같았다. 아, 그럴 수만 있다면, 삼십 대 초반에 무슨 귀신처럼 달라붙어서 이십하고도 오륙 년을 더 보태야 하는 세월 동안에 날이 갈수록 더 집요해지고 더 모질어지는 병마도 고통도 홀홀 벗어던지고 원망도 미련도 없이 이승을 떠날 수 있을 것 같았다.

오줌 누는 자세를 잡은 익수가 깜박 보리 냄새를 잊어먹었다. 오줌 소리가 아내에게 들리게 해서는 안 된다. 이말을 웅얼거린 그는 오줌발을 요리조리 뿌리겠다는 요령을 주의사항처럼 똑바로 세웠다.

아침부터 정오까지 꼬박 바다에 잠겨 암초들의 틈바구니를 땅꾼처럼 헤집고 다니며 전복 해삼 참소라를 따서 중매상이나 식당에 넘기고 돌아선 즉시 집으로 달려와,

long period, Ik-su went to the back of his house and stared at the barley field. This year, though, something felt strange. The barley field was giving off the intense aroma of water boiled with lots of burnt rice. He wondered if the taste of something being roasted originally had a golden yellow color. He also felt as if his heart was being dyed golden yellow, like this taste. He also felt relieved, believing there would be a bounteous barley aroma in the other world as well, since death is supposed to be the other side of life. The same thought sometimes brought him a strange wish. If only he lay down on that lonely grave near the far end of the barley field —the spot where he created an unforgettable memory with Suk-hui under the faint moonlight one night in the distant past, when he was in his twenties—and died alone! He felt he could then have a great sense of achievement at the end of his life, having come full circle back to his most precious experience of happiness. *Ah, if only he could do that...* then, he could leave this world without any resentment or regret, shaking off the demon of illness and pain that had stuck to him in his early thirties like a ghost and had become more and more persistent and ruthless for more than twenty-five

자기 손으로 차린 점심상을 뚝딱 해치우기 바쁘게 통조림 공장의 통근버스에 몸을 싣는 여자. 이것이 숙희의 벗어날 수 없는 일상이다. 익수는 잘 알고 있다. 아내를 도울 수 있는 거의 유일한 수단이 밤의 평온한 휴식에 훼방 놓지 않는 것임을. 가족, 가정이란 공간에서 가장(家長)이란 자가 맡을 최선의 역할이 그뿐이었다. 이 사실이 그에게는 병마의 고통보다 더 견디기 힘든 고통이었다.

익수가 사각팬티를 내렸다. 뼈대만 앙상한 손가락이 남근을 잡자 마치 나무젓가락으로 말랑말랑한 오뎅 토막을 집는 듯했다.

"흐응."

오줌과 함께 쓴웃음이 떨어졌다. 온몸을 샅샅이 살펴봐도 제 꼴을 제대로 간직한 것이라곤 이 물건 하나밖에 없다는 확인이 새삼 그의 뇌리를 할퀸 것이었다. 얼굴, 팔, 다리, 배, 가슴, 엉덩이, 몸의 구석구석, 심지어 발바닥과 손등과 손바닥까지. 모든 지방질을 면도칼로 깡그리 긁어낸 것처럼 뼈다귀에 거죽만 붙은 익수의 신체 중 변함없는 꼴을 오달지게 지탱하고 있는 최후의 부위가 바로 거웃 속에 엄지발가락처럼 박힌 그것이었다. 더구나 부풀었다 줄었다 하는 기능까지 유지하고 있다.

years since.

Ready to urinate, Ik-su forgot the aroma of barley for a moment. *I shouldn't let the noise reach my wife's ears.* Mumbling, he reminded himself of his strict rule that he should sprinkle his urine here and there.

Suk-hui loaded her body onto the cannery commuter bus as soon as she had eaten the lunch she had prepared after running back home the moment she had finished selling the abalones, sea cucumbers, and turban shells she had picked from the reefs and underwater rocks like a snake catcher submerged in the sea all morning. That was the daily routine Suk-hui never failed to follow. Ik-su knew very well that probably the only thing he could do to help her was not disturb her peaceful sleep at night. That was the best role he could play as head of the household. This knowledge was even more painful to him than the pain of his illness.

Ik-su took down his shorts. His bony fingers holding his penis were like chopsticks holding a soft fish sausage.

"Huh-huh."

A bitter laugh dropped to the ground along with

톡, 톡, 톡. 그는 평생을 익혀 온 버릇대로 세 번 남근을 털고 나서, "흐옹. 흐옹." 거푸 쓴웃음을 날렸다. 어쩌다 한 번씩 아내를 뜨겁게 해 줄 수 있는 이놈의 도구를 소중히 간수해야 한다는 희떠운 맹세를 되뇌고는 스스로 어처구니가 없어진 것이었다. 간혹 아내를 안아 주는 것이 남편 노릇의 전부라니! 그가 야윈 주먹을 쥐었다. 내일 집에 다니러 온다는 큰놈이 다시 기도원으로 돌아간 뒤에는 보리밭의 그 무덤가로 가서 영원히 잠들고 말겠다는 다짐이 울컥 짜증처럼 치밀었다.

깜박, 깜박, 깜박……. 기다란 방파제의 끄트머리를 지켜선 무인(無人) 등대에는 오직 한 톨의 불빛이 규칙적으로 줄기차게 명멸하고 있었다. 거대한 어둠의 도가니 속에 홀로 살아남은 외톨의 반딧불이 같은 그것을 익수는 보지 못했다.

"뭐 하러 나갔어요? 세 시도 안 됐던데."

익수가 살금살금 쪽마루에 올라서는데 방 안에서 조금 나무라는 목소리가 나왔다. 순간, 그는 어쩔 줄 몰랐다. 낭패감이 덮친 것이었다.

"잠이 안 오던가요?"

"아니. 오줌 누고 온다. 내가 단잠을 깨웠지? 잘 밤에

18

his urine. He was excruciatingly reminded that his penis was the only thing that was still normal of all his parts, from his face to his arms, legs, belly, chest, butt, every nook and cranny of his body, even his soles, the backs of his hands, and his palms. The last part that maintained its normal health in Ik-su's skin-and-bones body, a body that looked as if all the fat had been thoroughly sliced from it with a razor blade, was that thing lodged like a big toe within his pubic hair. In addition, it still even possessed its function of swelling and shrinking.

Tok, tok, tok. After shaking it three times as he had been doing all his life, he laughed bitterly, "Huh-huh." He felt ridiculous after reminding himself of his own vain promise that he should take good care of this tool that could make his wife excited once in a while. *To make love to his wife once in a while is the only thing he can do as a husband!* He made a fist with his skeletal hand. Annoyed, he suddenly remembered his promise to himself that he would go to that grave near the barley field and sink into eternal rest after his eldest son, who announced that he would visit the next day, went back to the prayer house.

수박을 먹지 말 걸."

올수박이 나왔더라며 아내가 낑낑 들고 온 그놈을, 그
가 아홉 시 뉴스를 보면서 몇 조각 먹긴 먹었다.

"깨우기는요. 당신 나가는 거 다 알았어요. 소피보러 가
는 줄 알았으면 요강에 누라고 했지요. 어슬어슬한데 문
닫고 잡시다."

"그러자. 감기 들겠다."

익수는 방문을 닫고 아내 옆에 누웠다.

"영호가 뭐 하러 온다고 그러는지 짐작이 안 가네요. 집
에 다녀가라고 사정을 해도 싫다던 애가, 참."

"그냥 한번 가족이 보고 싶어졌는지도 모르잖아? 영호
한테는 말을 못 해 줬는데, 일주일 뒤에 다시 온다고 한
그 기자한테도 잘됐지 뭐."

오랜만에 아들이 집에 다니러 온다는데 어머니가 얄궂
은 일이나 생긴 것처럼 근심부터 앞세우느냐. 이 불만을
익수는 삼켜버렸다.

어제 오후 2시쯤이었다. 늘 그렇듯 그맘때는 혼자서 집
을 지키는 익수가 기도원에 사는 영호의 전화를 받았다.
아버지와 아들의 통화는 제법 장난스러웠다. "보리밭이
완전히 황금색으로 물들었지요?" "밭주인들은 타작 날을

Blink, blink, blink... A beam of light was flickering regularly and persistently from the unmanned lighthouse standing guard at the farthest tip of a long breakwater. Ik-su did not notice that light, a lonely firefly, the only survivor in the crucible of darkness.

"What were you doing outside? It's not even three yet."

A scolding voice came from the bedroom as he was quietly climbing back onto the narrow veranda. He froze. He felt so frustrated.

"You couldn't sleep?"

"No, I went out to pee. I woke you up, didn't I? I wish I hadn't eaten watermelon this evening."

Watching the nine o'clock news, Ik-su ate a few pieces of the heavy watermelon his wife had lugged home with great effort. She said it was among the first batch of watermelons this season.

"You, wake me up? I knew you were going out. If I knew you were going out to pee, I would have told you to use the chamber pot. It's chilly. Let's close the door and sleep."

"OK. We don't need to catch cold."

After closing the door, Ik-su lay down next to his wife.

"I wonder why Yeong-ho is coming home. What's

받고 있을 거다." "뒷산 뻐꾸기는 잘 울고 있지요?" "그
래. 마침 울고 있는데, 들어볼래?" 익수가 송수화기를 뒷
산 쪽으로 맞추는 시늉을 했다. "희미하게 들리네요." "그
동네는 뻐꾸기도 안 우나?" "울어봤자 고향 뻐꾸기만 못
합니다." "노인네 같은 소리를 한다." "내일, 고향 뻐꾸기
소리 들으러 갑니다. 오후 3시쯤 도착합니다."

반듯이 누웠으니 엉덩이뼈가 아려오는 익수는 몸을 돌
리고 싶다. 왼팔도 편안히 아내의 가슴에 걸치고 싶다. 그
러나 주저하고 있었다. 괜히 아내의 몸을 달구면 어쩌나.
이 야박한 계산의 경계심에 짓눌리는 것이었다. 익수와
숙희의 부부관계는 열흘 간격이다. 거의 수칙 같은 그것
에 따르면 아직 사흘 여유가 남았다. 하지만 그는 머리가
좀 복잡했다. 내일은 안방을 같이 써야 하는 큰놈이 온다
지 않는가. 오늘은 아랫방의 작은놈도 나가고 없지 않는
가. 지금이야말로 그냥 지나갈 수 없지 않는가. 그러나 그
는 자신감이 일지 않았다. 남편 구실의 최후 능력을 발휘
하느라 격렬한 몸짓에 몰두하다가는 허리뼈가 부러질 것
같았다.

익수가 얌전히 몸을 반대로 돌렸다. 아내에게 등을 주
는 자세였다. 숙희는 더 이상 기다릴 수 없다고 생각했다.

happened to that son of ours who always said 'no' even when we begged him to visit?"

"Maybe he just misses his family. I didn't have a chance to tell Yeong-ho, but it's good timing since that reporter said he'd come by in a week."

When our son visits after such a long time, why are you, his mother, worried that something awful must be happening? Ik-su swallowed this complaint and sent it down his throat.

Around two P.M. yesterday, Ik-su, alone at home as usual, got a call from Yeong-ho who was at the prayer house, where he lived. They bantered lightly. "The barley field must be completely golden by now, right, Father?" "I bet the owners of barley fields have set the date for threshing." "Are the cuckoos on the hill behind our house still crying?" "Yes, they're crying right now. Do you want to listen?" Ik-su moved the receiver to face the hill. "I can hear it faintly." "There aren't any cuckoos in your village?" "There are, but they don't cry like the cuckoos at home." "You sound like an old man." "I'll come home tomorrow to listen to the cuckoos there. I'll arrive around three P.M."

Lying on his back, Ik-su wanted to turn over: his hip was hurting because his hipbone was touching

말을 먼저 거느냐, 몸을 먼저 건드리느냐. 이럴까 저럴까 밀고 당기는 가운데 자신도 모르게 몸이 돌아갔다.

"여보, 잠들었어요?"

숙희의 오른손이 펄쩍 뛰어 남편의 어깨에 올라붙었다. 뒤에서 껴안는 모양새가 거의 완성되었다.

"아니다. 잠이 안 오네. 그래도 자 보자."

숙희는 파르르 떨었다. 몸에 좁쌀이 돋았다.

"여보, 이리로 좀 돌아누워요. 당신 왜 이래요? 그저께 밤에도, 어젯밤에도 나를 색이나 밝히는 나쁜 년으로 만들던데, 당신한테서 기적을 확인하고 싶은 줄 알아요?"

숙희가 뇌리에 파편처럼 박힌 '기적'이란 말을 빼냈다. 기적, 그랬다. 분명히 그것은 익수의 단어였다. 달포 전, 꼭두새벽. 모처럼 흥건한 부부관계를 마친 남편이 허허로운 웃음과 함께 날린 한마디. 내가 아직 거기는 성한 게 기적 같구나.

"이 사람이 왜 이러나?"

익수가 몸을 돌렸다. 모로 누운 부부가 얼굴을 맞대었다.

"당신 나한테 크게 화나 있지요?"

"화를 내다니?"

the floor through the futon. He wanted to put his left arm across his wife's breast. But he was hesitating. *What if that ends up making my wife horny?* This cautious and coldhearted calculation made him think twice. Ik-su and Suk-hui made love every ten days. According to this regular schedule, they had three more days to go. But he was pondering some complicated logistics. *Tomorrow our eldest son will come home, and he'll have to share our bedroom. Besides, our youngest son isn't home tonight. I shouldn't pass up this opportunity.* Yet he didn't feel up to it. He was afraid he might break his spine while making passionate love to his wife in order to play his last remaining role as her husband.

Ik-su gently turned around with his back against Suk-hui. Suk-hui was becoming impatient. She couldn't wait any longer. While she was wavering between talking to him first and touching his body first, she turned toward him unawares.

"Honey, are you sleeping?"

Suk-hui's hand jumped onto Ik-su's shoulder. She seemed to be hugging him from behind.

"No, I can't fall asleep. But let's try to sleep."

Suk-hui was getting angry. She felt covered with gooseflesh.

"당신보고 밥벌레라 했으니……."

숙희가 훌쩍 콧물을 빨았다.

"그거 생각하느라고 잠도 못 잤나? 다 안다."

익수가 언 손에 입김을 불어주듯 속삭였다. 숙희는 온
몸을 들썩이고 있었다.

"내 마음은 절대로 그게 아닌데……."

"이 사람이야, 혼자서 걱정을 키워 가지고는 이러네."

"어째 그 말이 그렇게도 쉽게 튀어나왔는지……."

익수가 아내의 베개와 어깨 사이의 빈 공간으로 야윈
팔뚝을 넣고 젖은 얼굴을 깡마른 가슴에 품었다.

"여보, 너무 미안해요."

"그걸 이틀씩이나 속에 가두고 있었나? 쓸데없는 생각,
쓸데없는 소리는 다 쫓아버려라. 나는 아무렇지도 않다."

한 손으로 아내의 촉촉한 등을 어루만지는 익수의 눈앞
에 그저께 저녁에 보았던 텔레비전 뉴스가 되살아나고 있
었다.

*

기자가 익수를 찾아왔다. 그의 생애에 처음 생긴 일이

26

"Honey, please turn toward me. Why are you act-ing like this? You treated me like a bitch that's only interested in sex last night and the night before. Do you think I just want to confirm that miracle again?"

Suk-hui mentioned "miracle," a word lodged in her brain like a splinter. *Miracle, that's right.* It was true that Ik-su used that word. At dawn about a fort-night ago, he said, with a bitter laugh, after an espe-cially passionate session of lovemaking, *it's like a miracle that I'm still fine down there!*

"What's wrong?"

Ik-su turned around. They were facing each other.

"Aren't you really angry with me?"

"Angry?"

"I called you a useless mouth..."

Suk-hui was sniveling.

"You haven't fallen asleep just because of that? I know that's not what you meant," Ik-su whispered affectionately, as if blowing upon her frozen hands. Suk-hui's entire body kept shuddering.

"I didn't really mean it..."

"Honey, why are you making such a big deal out of it?"

"How easily that word came out of my mouth..."

Ik-su put his scrawny arm through the space

었다. 카메라를 어깨에 짊어진 젊은이와 역학조사 경험이 많다는 의사가 동행했다. 기자는 호리호리하고 의사는 뚱뚱했다. 익수는 여남은 살 아래의 낯선 두 사내에게 베트남에서 화학무기 다뤘던 경험들을 털어놓았다. 오전 10시에 못 미쳐 나타난 그들은 정오를 한참 지나서 일어섰다. 방송사의 부탁에 따라 물질을 쉬는 숙희가 점심을 차리려 했다. 그들은 사양했다. 답례는 있었다. 의사가 청진기로 그의 쌕쌕대는 숨소리를 들어줬고, 기자는 오늘 밤 전국 뉴스에 선생님네가 보훈의 달을 기념하는 특집뉴스로 나갈 것이라며 얇은 봉투를 내놓았다.

익수, 숙희, 공고(工高) 2학년 영섭. 세 식구는 저녁 9시 직전에 시험 문제지를 기다리는 수험생처럼 안방의 텔레비전 앞에 모여 있었다. 익수네는 네 번째 뉴스였다.

"고엽제 후유증으로 각종 질병에 시달리는 베트남 참전용사가 있습니다. 보도에……."

앵커가 사라지고 마이크를 잡은 호리호리한 기자가 들어서더니 홀연히 허름한 방 복판에 얼룩무늬 반팔남방 차림의 중년 사내 하나가 앉아 있다. 광대뼈가 뒤꿈치처럼 툭 불거지고 두 눈은 그것을 끼울 만큼 움푹 꺼진 얼굴이 화면을 가득 채운다. 한 발 떨어져 숨을 죽이고 지켜보는

between her pillow and shoulder and drew her wet face into his shrunken chest.

"I'm so sorry, honey," said Suk-hui.

"You've been thinking about that for two days? Nonsense! Forget all that nonsense! I don't care at all."

The TV news program Ik-su had watched two nights before came alive before his eyes while he was patting his wife's damp back.

*

A reporter visited Ik-su for the first time. This young man lugging a camera was accompanied by a doctor known for his experience in epidemiology. The reporter was slender and the doctor chubby. Ik-su told these two strangers, both some ten years younger, how he had handled chemical weapons during the Vietnam War. They came a little before ten A.M. and left well past noon. Suk-hui was home, taking the morning off from her diving work at the request of the broadcasting company. She offered them lunch, but they politely refused. There was a reward. The doctor listened to Ik-su's panting with a stethoscope, and the reporter gave him a thin

29

익수는 저게 누구인지 스스로 너무 낯설다. 차라리 보지 말 걸. 개구리처럼 펄쩍 뛰어 텔레비전을 꺼버리고 싶다. 그러나 잔뜩 눈살만 찌푸리고 있다.

"더욱 놀랄 일은 2세에도 고엽제 후유증의 유전으로 추정되는 심각한 증상이 나타나고 있다는 사실입니다."

엎드려 있는 영호가 등장한다. 오후에는 복음기도원을 찾아가겠다던 기자가 기어코 부지런을 떨었던 모양이다. 영호는 지시에 따르는 듯이 고개를 세운다. 그저 무덤덤한 표정이다. 익수가 눈을 감는다. 짐짓 외면을 하건만 귀는 닫히지 않는다.

그는 보도의 관점이 거슬렸다. 2세에 더 초점을 맞춘 것이 불쾌하다. '낙엽살초제'도 취급했지만 '씨에스파우더'를 더 많이 만졌다는 강조를 쏙 빼먹은 것이 섭섭하고 꽤씸하다.

"잘 보세요!" 익수가 놀란다. 화면에 아내가 나와 있다. 짠물에 절은 시커먼 얼굴에 유난히 눈알이 반들거린다. "목숨만 붙어 있다 뿐이지 해골입니다! 산 송장이지요, 산 송장! 밥벌레지요, 밥벌레! 죽음도 무섭다고 비켜가는 밥벌레! 우리는 너무너무 억울해서……."

누군가를 물어뜯을 기세였으나 이내 목이 막힌다. 익수

envelope, saying that there would be special coverage of Ik-su's family in commemoration of Veteran's Month.

The family of three—Ik-su, Suk-hui, and Yeong-seop, a junior in high school—gathered in front of the TV set just before nine P.M. like students eagerly awaiting the distribution of exams. Ik-su's story was the fourth news item.

"There is a Vietnam War veteran who is suffering from various illnesses as a result of handling defoliants in Vietnam. Reporter..."

The anchor disappeared, a slender reporter appeared with a microphone in his hand, and then suddenly there was a middle-aged man wearing a polka-dotted short-sleeve shirt in the center of a shabby room. A close-up shot of his cheekbones protruding like heels and his eyes, so sunken that heels could fit into them, filled the screen. The face looked so strange to Ik-su, watching at some distance from the others while holding his breath, that he wondered who that person was. *I wish I weren't watching this!* He wanted to jump to the TV set like a frog and turn it off. But he just kept frowning, hard.

"Even more alarming is that the second generation

는 아내가 처참히 비친 것이 억울하다. 다시 눈을 감는다. 단번에 끝낸 아내의 인터뷰에 대한 기자의 칭찬이 생생히 들려온다.

"아주머니의 그 절규가 고엽제 환자와 가족들에게 큰 도움이 될 것입니다."

"네에. 전쟁이란 이렇게 참혹한 것입니다."

익수의 귀에는 기자의 칭찬과 앵커의 결론이 겹쳐졌다. 그가 뒤로 물러나서 벽에 등을 기댄다. 어지럽다. 팔다리가 해파리처럼 허물거리는 느낌이다. 숙희는 말없이 화면을 노려보고, 영섭은 고개를 떨어뜨리고 있다. 뉴스의 꼬리를 뉴스가 물고 또 문다. 누가 누구를 죽이고, 누가 누구를 속여먹고, 누가 누구를 성추행하고, 누가 누구를 잡아 가두고……. 피비린내와 구린내를 앞장세운 사람살이의 온갖 잡동사니들이 익수네 꾀죄죄한 안방에 넘쳐난다. 불현듯 마당이 웅성웅성 살아난다.

"익수, 뭐하나?"

"대통령보다 길게 나왔다. 오늘 저녁에는 자네가 대한민국 대통령이었다."

"우리 동네도 출세했다."

이웃들이다. 동네에 경사가 생긴 것처럼 들떠 있다. 서

is also suffering from serious symptoms, which are, doctors suppose, the transmitted aftereffects of defoliant usage."

Yeong-ho appeared, lying face down. The reporter, who said he was planning to visit the prayer house, must have been diligent enough to go there. Yeong-ho raised his head, probably in response to a request. He looked calm. Ik-su closed his eyes. Although he deliberately looked away, he couldn't help hearing. He didn't like the angle of this report. He was disturbed by the focus on the second generation. He was also saddened and angered by the omission of the fact, which he had made clear, that he handled CS powder even more than defoliants.

"Look at him carefully!" Ik-su was suddenly jolted. His wife was on screen. Her eyes were shining brightly in her salted, dark face. "He's a virtual skeleton! Practically a dead body, right, a dead body! A useless mouth, you know, a useless mouth! A useless mouth that even death fears and avoids! This is so unjust..."

She looked about to bite somebody, but she was choking up. Ik-su didn't like his wife looking so miserable. He closed his eyes again. He vividly

넛은 서슴없이 쪽마루에 걸터앉는다.

"뭡니까? 불난 집에 부채질합니까! 내가 텔레비전에 나
가면 사람이 아니다! 나는 죽어도 안 나간다!"

벌떡 일어서서 고함을 지른 영섭이 성난 황소처럼 뛰쳐
나간다.

"섭아!"

"놔둬라."

익수가 아내를 말린다. 숙희가 외등 스위치를 올린다.

"비좁지만 마루에 올라앉으세요. 기자가 들고 온 주스
가 있어요. 우리 섭이는 화가 나서 그럽니다. 기자가 다시
온다고 했는데, 습진 같은 게 생겨서는 아무리 약을 발라
도 차도는 없고 오히려 심해지고 있으니 혹시나 해서
는……."

숙희가 아들의 무례에 대한 변호를 하다가 말을 맺지
못한다. 익수는 잘 알고 있다. 영섭의 사타구니에 흔한 습
진으로 보이는 것이 생겨나서 연고를 네 통이나 발랐으나
자꾸 덧나고 있다. 아버지의 몹쓸 병을 물려받은 게 아닌
가. 아들과 아내는 불안해 하고 있다. 내 몹쓸 병을 작은놈
한테도 물려준 게 아닌가. 아버지는 가슴을 졸이고 있다.

heard the reporter praising his wife, who had done the interview on his first try.

"Her cry will be a great help to all patients suffering from defoliants, and their families."

"Yes, this is the cruelty of war."

The reporter's praise and the anchor's conclusion were overlapping in Ik-su's ears. He moved backward toward the wall, still sitting, and leaned against it. He felt dizzy. His arms and legs felt listless, like jellyfish. Suk-hui was silently glaring at the screen, and Yeong-seop was hanging his head. More news kept following: So-and-so killed such-and-such, so-and-so deceived such-and-such, so-and-so sexually harassed such-and-such, and so-and-so arrested and imprisoned such-and-such... All the bloody, stinking details of human lives were flowing into Ik-su's shabby bedroom. All of a sudden, his yard came alive. It was abuzz.

"Ik-su, what are you doing?"

"Your story was longer than the president's. You were the president tonight."

"Our village made it onto the world stage, too."

Neighbors were all in high spirits as if this was some happy occasion. A few did not even hesitate to perch on the narrow veranda.

*

땡볕이 내리쬐는 호미곶의 나른한 적요 속으로 뻐꾸기
울음소리가 아스라이 번져 나가고 있었다. 뻐어꾸욱, 뻐
어꾸욱, 뻐어꾸욱. 익수는 옴나위없는 덫에 걸린 것처럼
꼼짝없이 담벼락에 기대앉아 그 울음소리를 듣고 있었다.
뻐어꾸욱, 집 뒤. 뻐어꾸욱, 보리밭 너머. 뻐어꾸욱, 뒷산
어느 솔가지. 심심파적으로 뻐꾸기의 위치를 더듬던 그가
조용히 탄식을 내고 말았다.

"용케도 돌아와서 또 저렇게 울어 주는구나."

호미곶의 보리밭이 황금빛으로 물드는 무렵에는 어김
없이 뻐꾸기가 돌아와서 줄기차게 울어대고, 익수는 그
절기를 못 넘기고 요강이 골싹하도록 선혈을 게워낸 뒤
주검과 진배없는 상태로 응급실에 실려 갔다. 그것은 지
난 십여 년 동안에 해마다 한 차례씩 잔혹한 연중행사로
반복되었다. 죽음의 예행 연습 같았다.

"푸우—."

익수가 한숨을 몰아내면서 왼손을 눈앞으로 들어올렸
다. 손목에 있던 시계가 뼈다귀뿐인 팔뚝을 타고 내려와
팔꿈치에 걸렸다. 베트남에서 박문현 대위가 작별의 선물

36

"What are you doing? Are you pouring salt in our wounds? If I ever do an interview for TV, I'm not a human being! I will never do that!" After abruptly standing up and yelling, Yeong-seop stormed out of the house like an angry bull.

"Seop!"

"Leave him alone!"

Ik-su stopped his wife. Suk-hui switched on the outdoor lamp.

"Please come inside, although the room is so small. The reporter brought us some juice. Seop is behaving like that because he's angry. The reporter said he'd come again. Seop is suffering from something like eczema, which no ointment seems to cure. It's getting worse, so..."

Trying to apologize for her son's rude behavior, Suk-hui couldn't finish her words. Ik-su knew very well what was going on. Something like eczema had been developing in Yeong-seop's groin and was getting worse despite four tubfuls of ointment. *Maybe he inherited my dreadful disease?* Both his son and wife were worried. *Maybe I transmitted that frightful disease even to my youngest son.* Ik-su was anxious and worried.

로 건네준 일제 세이코. 전쟁의 상처처럼 악독하게도 늙을 줄 모르고 지칠 줄 모르는 시계가 3시에 다가서고 있었다. 영호가 도착할 시간이었다.

익수는 뒤통수를 담벼락에 붙였다. 따끈한 기운이 목덜미를 타고 내렸다. 영호를 의식한 탓일까. 얼핏 뻐꾸기 따위에 운명을 맡기지 않겠다는 삶의 의욕 같은 무엇이 미물처럼 꼬물꼬물 일고 있었다. 그것이 움푹 파인 두 눈을 찡그리게 했다. 이층짜리 누런 횟집과 하얀 모텔 사이에 파란 바다가 큼직한 빨래처럼 걸려 있었다. 그 서너 발 길이의 수평선을, 그의 시선은 또렷이 포착했다. 아직 시력은 정상이구나. 그가 가녀린 미소를 지으며 시선을 거두어 시계를 만지작거렸다. 박문현 대위와 만난 것이 내 운명이었단 말인가. 익수는 얼굴에 햇볕을 쪼이려는 듯이 고개를 뒤로 젖혔다.

*

1964년 12월 1일. 김익수는 대한민국 육군에 입대했다. 22세, 체중 68kg, 신장 172cm. 논산훈련소 6주와 대전통신학교 2주를 거친 뒤 철책선 수색중대에 떨어졌으나 다

The cuckoos' cries were seeping far and wide into the languid stillness under the hot sun. *Cuckoo, cuckoo, cuckoo.* Ik-su listened to those crying sounds, leaning against the wall helplessly, as if imprisoned in a trap with no wiggle room whatsoever. *Cuckoo,* behind his house. *Cuckoo,* over the farthest end of the barley field. *Cuckoo,* from a branch of pine on the hill behind his house. Trying to guess where the cuckoos were calling from, just to kill time, Ik-su quietly grieved, "How marvelous! They've returned as always and cry as always."

Whenever the barley fields turned golden, the cuckoos never failed to return and cry. Whenever this happened, Ik-su also never failed to vomit enough blood to almost fill the chamber pot, and be taken to the emergency room like a dead body. For the previous ten years, this had happened like some annual ritual. It felt like a rehearsal for death.

"Whew~" Sighing deeply, Ik-su raised his left arm and held it in front of his eyes. The watch on his wrist was slipping further and further down his thin arm toward his elbow. It was a Seiko watch made in Japan, a farewell gift from Capt. Bak Mun-hyeon

시 1군 화학학교 CBR하사관 반에 차출당해 화학병 교육을 받았다.

베트남전쟁, 그때 한국인이 '월남전'이라 부른 전쟁터로 가려고 익수가 장기 복무를 자원한 것은 병장 말년이었다. 제대특명을 한 달 앞두면 예비특명을 먼저 받게 되는데, 그 직전에 그는 엉뚱한 결심을 했다. 무엇보다 한밑천 단단히 거머쥐게 될 것이란 기대감이 앞서 있었다.

부산항을 떠나는 김익수 병장의 체중은 70kg이었다. 그의 전우들을 태운 함정은 아흐레 만엔가 베트남 퀴논에 닿았다. 환한 대낮이었다. 평화로운 상륙작전을 엘브이티가 전담했다. 그는 호기심과 두려움이 뒤섞여 두근두근 뛰는 가슴으로 베트남 땅에 첫발을 놓았다.

맹호사단 연병장에서 신고식을 마친 익수는 1연대에 배속되었다. 연대 교육훈련소는 퀴논 시 외곽의 푸칼에 있었다. 베트남 신병들은 한 주일에 걸쳐 기본 교육을 받았다. 실제 매복, 야간 도보, 정글 통과, 정훈 교육 따위로 짜인 과정이었다.

기본 교육 나흘째, 정훈 교육 시간이었다. 장교가 김익수 병장을 따로 불러냈다. 강 아무개 대위였다. 수송관이란 그가 다짜고짜 선언했다.

in Vietnam. Never aging or tiring, unlike his war-wounded body, the watch was pointing to nearly three P.M. Yeong-ho was about to arrive.

Ik-su leaned the back of his head against the wall. Warmth was flowing down through the nape of his neck. Perhaps because he was thinking of Yeong-ho, something like a will to live, a resolution that he wouldn't leave his fate to the hands of such a small thing as a cuckoo, was wriggling in his mind like a tiny microorganism. That sheer force of will made him frown, the skin crinkling around his two sunken eyes. The blue sea was hanging like washed clothes on a string between a yellowish two-story sushi restaurant and a white motel. He caught sight of the horizon stretching for several fathoms. *My eyesight is still fine.* Faintly smiling, he started fumbling with his watch. *Was it my fate to meet Capt. Bak Mun-hyeon?* Ik-su leaned back as if he wanted to feel the warmth of the sun on his face.

*

Kim Ik-su enlisted in the Korean Army on December 1, 1964. Age: 22, weight: 68kg, height: 172cm. He was first assigned to a border search

"너, 사회에서 택시 했잖아? 신상카드는 장난으로 만든 게 아냐. 너, 내가 수송부로 데려간다. 임마, 땡 잡은 거야. 이 남국에서 드라이브나 즐기다가 딸라 챙겨 가지고 돌아가게 되는 거야."

익수는 어리둥절했다. 입대하기 전에 여섯 달쯤 '새나라'라는 일제 택시를 몰았던 것이 뒤늦게 엄청난 행운을 안겨줄 줄이야 꿈엔들 생각했겠는가. 그런데 5분 지나지 않아서 다른 장교가 또 익수를 불러냈다. 박문현 대위였다. 날카로운 첫인상답게 그가 단호히 명령했다.

"김익수, 너는 누가 와서 묻든지 간에 화학밖에 모른다고 해. 운전이니 뭐니 하면 차는 멀미 때문에 타 본 적도 없는 거야. 알겠어?"

익수는 냉큼 대답을 못 했다. 그러나 박 대위의 군홧발이 날아들진 않았다. 그를 미행한 것처럼 강 대위가 끼어든 것이었다. 두 장교가 챙챙 말다툼을 벌였다.

"위에 가서 알아 봐? 누가 옳은지? 김익수가 현지 창녀야? 먼저 찍으면 임자게."

박 대위가 큰소리를 뺑뺑 치고 나가니까 강 대위가 체면 유지 선에서 꼬리를 사렸다. 익수는 나중에야 깨달았지만 육사(陸士)가 비육사를 깔아뭉갠 한판이었다.

company after six weeks of training at the Nonsan Recruit Training Center and two weeks of training at the Daejeon Communication School. But he was soon selected to join the CBR non-commissioned officer class at the First Army Chemical School and was trained as a chemical technician.

In his last year as sergeant, Ik-su volunteered to extend his service so he could participate in the Vietnam War, the battleground Koreans at the time called 'Wolnamjeon.' He made this extravagant decision right before the preliminary special order that came a month before his discharge special order. He was hoping above all to earn some money by serving in Vietnam.

He weighed 70kg when he left the port of Busan. The warship carrying him and his fellow soldiers arrived in Qui Nhon, Vietnam after about a nine-day voyage. It was broad daylight when they arrived. An LVT awaited, part of a peaceful landing operation. His heart thumping with curiosity and fear, Ik-su landed on the soil of Vietnam.

After the reporting ceremony at the Maengho (Ferocious Tiger) Division drill ground, Ik-su was assigned to the 1st regiment. The Regiment Training Center was located in Phu Cat in the suburb of Qui

기본 교육을 수료한 익수는 열흘쯤 지나서 머리에 털 생기고 처음 헬기를 탔다. 미군 기갑사단으로 가서 실전 화학병 교육을 받게 된다고, 조종사 옆에 탄 박 대위가 일러줬다. 익수의 눈에는 공중에서 내려다보는 베트남 땅이 온통 잔디밭으로 보였다. 푸른 지상낙원 같았다. 그의 착시가 생뚱맞진 않았던 것일까. 영문과를 다니다 입대했다는, 그의 졸병으로 들어와 행정 실무를 맡은 상병도 처음 헬기를 타보고 나서 이런 소감을 털어놓았다. 하늘에서 내려다보면 평화의 잔디밭 같으니까 하늘에 계신 아버지께서는 베트남에 대해선 걱정도 안 할 것 같았습니다.

익수가 미군에 가서 배운 기술은 가스통에 장착할 폭파 장치 조작법, 네임판탄 조작법, 화염방사기 조작법 등이었다. 그의 특기는 눈이었다. 영어엔 귀머거리요 벙어리였으나 까다로운 폭파 장치도 한 번 눈으로 보았다 하면 기똥차게 재현했다. 통역처럼 지켜보는 박 대위가 싱글벙글 칭찬을 늘어놓을 수준이었다.

"코쟁이들이 김 병장의 눈썰미와 손재주에 탄복하는 거야. 원더풀을 연발하잖아? 그게 그 소리야. 그런 너를 골라잡았으니 나도 보통 행운이 아닌 거지."

그는 무게도 잡았다.

Nhon. New arrivals got basic training for a week. The curriculum covered Real-life Ambush, Nighttime March, Jungle Passage, and Troop Information and Education.

On the fourth day of this training, during the Troop Information and Education class, an officer called Sgt. Kim Ik-su aside. This was Capt. Kang, the transportation officer. He abruptly declared, "You've driven taxi as a civilian, right? Your personnel card isn't a trivial thing, you know. You're going to work in the transportation department. Hey, you should know that you're extremely lucky! You'll enjoy driving in this southern country and go back home with bags full of dollars."

Ik-su was at a loss. He worked as a taxi driver for only six months just before he enlisted, driving the "Saenara (New Nation)" made in Japan. He had never even dreamed that this career would bring him good luck. But then, in less than five minutes, another officer called him aside. This was Capt. Bak Mun-hyeon. A man who made a very sharp first impression, he authoritatively ordered Ik-su, "Kim Ik-su, if anybody comes and asks you, you should tell him that the only thing you know is chemistry. If somebody mentions driving or something, then

"김 병장, 너와 나는 여기서 한국군 최초의 화학 작전을 하게 되는 거야. 전사에 길이 남을 수 있어. 긍지를 가져야 해."

직속상관의 흐뭇한 표정에 익수는 어깨를 우쭐거렸다.

*

문득 골목길이 시끄럽다. 나른한 적요가 망가진다. 그는 잠자코 기다리기로 한다. 회색 승합차가 비틀비틀 올라오고 있다. 그가 속에 고인 공기를 뿜는다. 고무풍선의 주둥이로 빠져나가는 바람 소리 같다. 승합차가 그의 발치 밑 멍석만 한 빈터에서 짧은 전진과 후진을 반복한다. 설날 앞에 영호를 데려왔을 때도 그러더니, 운전기사는 돌아갈 마음이 바쁜지 차부터 돌려세우고 있다.

익수가 일어섰다. 영호보다 몇 살 더 먹었을 건장한 체구가 운전석에서 내려 중간 도어의 손잡이를 잡았다. '복음기도원'의 '도원'이 가려졌다. 별안간 예리한 것이 익수의 눈을 찔렀다. 차에서 꺼낸 휠체어의 금속이 반사한 햇빛.

"그렇지. 휠체어가 먼저 내리지."

익수가 허탈하게 중얼거렸다. 전혀 새삼스러울 것이 없

you should tell him that you haven't even ridden in a car because of carsickness. Got it?"

Ik-su couldn't answer right away. But Capt. Bak didn't even have the chance to kick him with his combat boots. Capt. Kang immediately showed up, as if he had been shadowing Ik-su. The two officers quarreled loudly.

"Do you want to check with our superiors? Who's right? Is Kim Ik-su some local prostitute? Whoever has his eye on him first gets him?" As Capt. Bak was making these wild claims, Capt. Kang just gave in, barely saving face. Ik-su later realized that this had been a fight in which a Military Academy graduate had trounced a non-Military Academy graduate.

About ten days after basic training, Ik-su flew in a helicopter for the first time. Capt. Bak, sitting next to the pilot in the cockpit, told Ik-su that he was going to get training as a chemical warfare soldier. To Ik-su, looking down from above, the land of Vietnam looked like an endless expanse of lawn, a green paradise on earth. Perhaps this optical illusion was not far off the mark... A private first class doing administrative duty, Ik-su's former subordinate who enlisted while studying English literature at college, said, after his first helicopter ride, *it seemed as if*

건만 가슴이 빠개지는 통증이 단전까지 뻗쳤다. 그랬다. 아버지는 여태껏 한 가닥의 희망을 차마 버리지 못하고 있었다. 언젠가 아들의 척수신경이 되살아날 것이라는.

운전기사가 익수를 쳐다보았다. 거들지 않고 왜 장승처럼 서 있는 거요. 꼭 그렇게 나무라는 것 같았다. 익수가 삭정이 같은 다리로 열댓 자죽을 내려가는 사이, 운전기사가 영호를 쌀자루처럼 껴안아서 휠체어에 앉혔다. 익수가 얼른 눈을 내리깔았다. 그 순간만은 아들의 시선을 피하고 싶었다.

"고생 많았지요? 고맙습니다."

익수는 아들보다 먼저 운전기사에게 인사를 건넸다.

"무슨 말씀을요. 반가운 소식이 있습니다. 근래에 들어서 영호 씨의 신앙심이 몰라보게 깊어졌습니다. 누구보다 기도에 열심입니다. 언젠가는 틀림없이 하나님의 은총이 임하실 겁니다."

그의 예언은 그의 건장한 육체처럼 건장한 것이었다.

"아버지, 뻐꾸기가 막 울음을 그쳤네요."

아버지를 쳐다보는 영호는 빙긋이 웃는 낯이었다.

"맞네. 줄기차게도 울어대더니. 울든 말든 나는 신경 안 쓴다."

God in heaven wasn't worried about Vietnam at all because it looked like a peaceful lawn from above. Ik-su learned from the U.S. Army how to operate an explosive device attached to a gas container, a napalm bomb, and a flamethrower. He learned with exceptional speed, just by observing I know it was a lot of trouble. Although he couldn't understand or speak a word of English, he could reproduce the process of operation for any device amazingly well, no matter how complicated. Watching nearby as a sort of interpreter, Capt. Bak kept smiling broadly and praising him. "Those big-noses are completely amazed at what a quick study you are, and your exceptional handiness. Didn't they keep saying 'wonderful'? That's what they meant. I was exceptionally lucky, too, in choosing you."

He then said, with a very serious tone, "Sgt. Kim, you and I are engaged in the first chemical warfare ever undertaken by the Korean Army. We'll go down in history forever. We should be proud!"

His immediate superior was so happy that Ik-su felt all puffed up, too.

익수가 휠체어 손잡이를 잡았다. 아들을 방문 앞에 데려가는 것까지 남의 손에 맡기기가 싫었다. 휠체어를 밀고 올라가면서 그는 뻐꾸기 따위에 운명을 맡기지 않겠다는 의욕을 확인해 본다. 그것이 휠체어 운전을 더욱 조심스럽게 만든다. 돌맹이 하나라도 애써 피한다. 덜컹, 하는 찰나에 이제 막 회생을 시작하려는 아들의 척수신경을 다칠세라, 그는 온 신경을 곤두세우고 있다.

*

재작년 이맘때였다. 그날도 뻐꾸기가 울었다. 거의 종일을 유난히도 청아하게 울었다. 호미곶 앞바다에 까치놀이 물들었을 때, 익수는 먹는 시늉만 내고 저녁상을 물렸다. 왠지 앉아 있을 기운조차 없었다. 일찌감치 자리에 누웠다. 아내가 설거지를 하는 동안에 그는 설핏 잠이 들었다. 밤이 깊어 갈수록 그의 잠도 깊어지고 있었다. 구덩이에 파묻힌 것 같은 잠에 빠졌던 그가 불현듯 눈을 떴다. 속이 느글느글 끓고 있었다.

"요강."

곧바로 익수는 요강이 골싹하도록 피를 게워냈다. 그리

*

The alley suddenly got noisy. The languid quiet dissipated. Ik-su decided to wait. A gray van was chugging toward him. Ik-su exhaled the air stagnating in his lungs. It sounded like air seeping out of the mouth of a balloon. The van started going forward and backward in a glade the size of a straw mat. As on New Year's Eve when the driver brought Yeong-ho home, he was busy turning the van around for his return trip.

Ik-su stood up. A robust man probably a few years older than Yeong-ho got down from the driver's seat and held the door handle in the middle, obscuring 'er House' from the name "Gospel Prayer House." Suddenly something sharp was piercing Ik-su's eyes. It was a beam of sunlight reflected off the metal of a wheelchair.

"That's right. The wheelchair has to get down first," Ik-su murmured with a sinking heart. Although there was nothing new about this, a heart-wrenching pain reached down into his belly. It was true that the father in him still couldn't give up hope, no matter how tenuous it was, that some day his son's spinal cord would revive.

고 빈사 상태로 응급실에 내려졌다. 잊지 않고 찾아온 죽음의 예행 연습이었다. 그런데 그가 일반 병실에 옮겨져서 사흘째 나는 아침이었다. 숙희가 남편의 병상에 한 손을 걸친 채 맥없이 주저앉았다.

"영호가요, 새벽에 눈을 뜨더니 하체가 말을 안 듣는다고 하대요. 지금 응급실에 와 있어요."

메마른 음성이었다. 한숨도 쉬지 않았다. 눈물도 짓지 않았다. 마치 오늘 새벽의 사태를 오랜 세월 기다려 온 사람처럼 체념하고 있었다. 붕어 비늘 같은 허연 입술에 착 달라붙은 머리칼 몇 올을 응시하는 익수의 눈가에 영롱한 이슬이 맺혔다.

아버지가 6층, 아들이 5층. 그러나 영호는 오래잖아 지방의 종합병원을 떠나갔다. 영세민 의료보험카드가 그를 서울 국립의료원으로 옮겨주었다. 영호의 정밀 진단을 맡았던 중년 의사가 숙희 앞에서 고개를 저었다.

"알 수 없는 일입니다. 최선을 다했지만 어떤 이상도 발견되지 않는군요. 그러니 수술을 시도할 수도 없어요. 솔직히, 의학적 호기심도 생깁니다만, 기적을 기원하는 수밖에 없을 것 같습니다."

의사는 환자에게도 사진을 보여주며 설명을 곁들였다.

The driver looked at Ik-su. *Why are you just standing there like a totem pole and not trying to help?* He seemed to be scolding Ik-su. While Ik-su was going down about fifteen steps, his legs like withered branches, the driver carried Yeong-ho like a bag of rice and sat him on the wheelchair. Ik-su immediately looked away. He wanted to avoid his son's eyes, at least at that moment.

"I know it was a lot of trouble for you. Thank you!" Ik-su thanked the driver before greeting his son.

"Not at all. I bring you good news. Recently Yeong-ho has become much more devout. He prays harder than anybody else. I'm sure that God's blessing will be with him someday." His prediction seemed as robust as his body.

"Father, a cuckoo just stopped crying." Smiling gently, Yeong-ho looked at his father.

"That's right, although they have been crying constantly. It doesn't matter to me whether they cry or not."

Ik-su took the handles of the wheelchair. He didn't want to rely on a stranger to take his son to the house. Pushing the wheelchair up the road, he remembered his resolution not to leave his fate to

현재로서는 원인을 규명하기 어렵다는 소견을 들은 영호가 눈을 둥그렇게 떴다.

"내 나이 스물두 살입니다. 여태까지 허리 아프다는 통증 한 번 느낀 적 없었는데 원인이 없다니, 그게 말이나 됩니까?"

의사가 겸연쩍게 대답했다.

"운이 나빴다고 생각하세요."

흑, 흑, 숨을 몰아쉰 영호가 울부짖었다.

"아버지—, 아버지—. 내가 나무를 죽였습니까, 베트콩을 죽였습니까! 그런데 내가 왜요, 아버지—."

베트남에서 돌아온 익수가 이태 뒤에 얻은 첫아들이 영호다. 영호가 초등학교에 들어간 그해부터 그는 일 년에 몇 차례씩 멀쩡히 앉아 있다가도 느닷없이 전신마비 증세를 일으켰다. 그런 경우에는 수십 분 동안 체온만 남은 시체로 살아 있었다.

숙희는 남편에게 하반신 마비의 아들을 기도원에 의탁하자고 했다. 익수는 아내의 의견을 하릴없이 수락했다. 생계를 책임지는 아내를 거들기는커녕 몇 푼 모아 놓기 바쁘게 한입에 홀랑 까먹고도 제 몸 하나 건사하지 못하는 주제에 다른 방안을 낼 재간이 없었다. 인체란 신비한

such trivial beings as cuckoos. This resolution made him even more careful while pushing the wheel-chair. He tried to avoid every tiny pebble. His nerves were on edge: he was afraid the wheelchair's thumping would hurt his son's spinal cord just at the moment it might be beginning to heal.

*

One day around this time two years earlier, the cuckoos were crying the same way. They had been crying with unusual clarity and elegance almost all day long. When the evening glow was dyeing the sea in front of Cape Homi, Ik-su stopped eating din-ner after a few spoonfuls. For some reason, he didn't even have the strength to sit up. He went to bed early. He dozed off while his wife was doing dishes. He was falling fast asleep, as the night was getting older. Suddenly he opened his eyes, awak-ened from a deep slumber that felt like being buried in a pit. He was feeling really sick.

"Chamber pot!"

Ik-su immediately vomited so much blood it almost filled the chamber pot to the brim. He was taken to the emergency room on the brink of death.

것이니 어느 날 갑자기 기적처럼 회복될 가능성이 없다고 단정할 수는 없습니다만, 어디까지나 하늘의 뜻에 달려 있습니다. 의사의 마지막 말을 숙희는 남편에게 전해줬다. 그것이 익수에게는 단순한 위로로 들리지 않았다. 희망의 끈 같았다. 그는 믿고 싶었다. 기도원이야말로 하늘과 가장 가까운 지상의 공간이라고.

*

"선풍기 틀어줄까?"

익수가 어렵사리 입을 열었다. 영호를 안방의 요 위에 눕혀준 운전기사가 돌아간 다음에 처음 거는 말이었다. 아버지는 속으로 아들에게 쩔쩔매고 있었다.

"괜찮은데요."

영호가 엎드린 자세에서 아버지를 쳐다보며 빙긋이 웃음을 지었다. 익수가 다른 화젯거리를 궁리하는 틈에 아들이 말을 건넸다.

"아버지는 유명해졌겠어요."

영호가 또 빙긋이 웃었다. 그것이 익수를 흠칫 놀라게 한다. 저 웃음이 뭐야? 징그럽게! 그러나 익수는 모른 척

It was the rehearsal for death that did not fail to visit him as usual. Then, on the third morning after he was hospitalized, Suk-hui collapsed listlessly, grasping his bed.

"It's Yeong-ho. Early this morning, he said he couldn't move from the waist down as soon as he opened his eyes. He's in the emergency room now."

Her voice was dry. She didn't even sigh. Or cry. She was resigned, like someone who had been waiting for this day for a long time. Around the edge of Ik-su's eyes teardrops were dangling like brilliant dewdrops, while he was staring at a few strands of her hair stuck to her pale lips like the scales of a crucian carp. Father on the sixth floor and son on the fifth. But Yeong-ho soon left that local hospital. A Medicare card for the poor made it possible for him to move to the National Medical Center in Seoul. A middle-aged doctor who did a close examination of Yeong-ho shook his head in front of Suk-hui.

"It's strange. Although I tried everything, I couldn't find any abnormalities. So we can't even try surgery. Frankly, I feel curious as a medical doctor, but there's nothing more to do except pray for a miracle."

한다.

"너도 보았지? 그 기자가 알려줬겠지."

"이런 주제에 뭐하자고 자꾸 뉴스는 보게 되네요."

이 세상에 의미 있는 게 무엇이냐고 묻는 것 같은 그 묘한 웃음을 영호는 빙긋이 머금고 있다. 익수는 다시 못 본 체했다. 농담을 하면 분위기가 나아질까? 그는 기대를 걸었다.

"겪어본 사람들은 알겠지만 유명해지는 것도 보통 어려운 일이 아니더라. 나도 장장 25년 넘는 세월이 안 걸렸나."

"그러니 아버지는 죽을 고비를 여러 번 넘기신 보람을 찾은 편이네요. 그것도 가족이 총출연을 했으니."

영호가 대뜸 받아넘기자 익수는 또 말문이 막혔다. 아들이 고개를 돌려 아버지를 외면했다. 아버지, 저의 하반신에 대한 집착을 버리세요. 익수는 그런 푸념을 들은 듯하다. 아버지는 무슨 대화든 더 나누려 한다. 그러나 아들이 휴대용 녹음기에 딸린 이어폰으로 귓구멍을 막아버린다.

*

익수와 영호는 첫날에 그랬듯이 이튿날에도 아침부터

The doctor explained this to Yeong-ho as well, showing him the X-rays. Yeong-ho's eyes widened after the doctor said he couldn't find a cause for his illness at that point.

"I'm only twenty-two. I have never even had a backache. How is it possible for you not to find any cause? Does that make sense?"

Embarrassed, the doctor said, "Please consider that you're particularly unlucky."

After taking deep breaths, *Whew, whew*, Yeong-ho cried and howled, "Father, father! Have I killed trees or Viet Cong? Why me? Father..."

Yeong-ho was Ik-su's first son, born two years after he returned from Vietnam. Ever since Yeong-ho entered elementary school, Ik-su would suddenly become completely paralyzed several times a year. He was a dead body for twenty to thirty minutes except that he was still warm.

Suk-hui proposed to entrust their son, paralyzed from the waist down, to the prayer house. Ik-su accepted this proposal helplessly. As someone who used up all the money as soon as his wife earned it, let alone someone who could not help her, he had no choice but to accept. *Although we cannot definitely say this won't be cured all of a sudden like a*

점심까지를 그저 데면데면하게 지냈다. 아버지는 잡념에, 아들은 녹음기에 열중한 시간들이었다. 할 일이라곤 그것뿐인 부자(父子) 같았다. 오후 2시가 넘었다. 허름한 방 안에 갯마을 한낮의 나른한 적요가 그득했다. 억지 쓰는 대화보다야 침묵이 수월하겠다고 결정한 아버지는 멀쩡하던 때의 아들과 지금 눈앞의 아들을 견줘보고 있었다.

영호는 엄전한 바탕에 사근한 구석을 갖춘 청년이었다. 철강공단에 취직한 뒤로는 퇴근길에 가끔 소주병과 삼겹살을 끼고 왔다. 조금만 취해 보시지요. 북어처럼 말라빠진 아버지에게 다정한 친구로 굴 줄도 알았다. 그러나 지금은 어떤가? 무뚝뚝하기 짝이 없다. 대화조차 피한다. 멀쩡한 시절의 엄전함이 지나치게 발달해서 어느덧 가슴마저 돌덩어리로 변한 것 같다. 다섯 달 만에 다니러 온 집인데 가족의 안부를 묻지 않았다. 동생이 전화도 없이 외박을 했으나 아예 무관심했다. 아버지와 어머니가 밥상머리에서 나흘째 외박한 영섭을 걱정했을 때, 그는 퉁명스레 쥐어박았다. 친구 집에 자겠지요. 아무것도 아닌 일로 뭘 그리 호들갑 떠느냐고 꾸지람한 것이었다.

익수는 동생에 대한 형의 태도가 새삼 야속해졌다. 지난 4월에 복음기도원을 다녀온 아내가 섭섭하게 듣지 말

miracle, that's all up to God. Suk-hui relayed these last words of the doctor to Ik-su. They weren't simply words of condolence. For Ik-su they were a thread of hope. He wanted to believe that the prayer house was the place closest to heaven on earth.

*

"Would you like me to turn on the fan?" Ik-su asked, hesitantly. This was his first attempt at conversation with his son since the driver had left, after he had placed Yeong-ho on the futon in the master bedroom. The father was flustered in front of his son.

"That's OK." Yeong-ho smiled, looking up at his father, while lying face down. While Ik-su was trying to think of some other topic to talk about, Yeong-ho said, "You must have gotten famous."

Yeong-ho smiled again. This smile surprised Ik-su. *What kind of smile is that? How creepy!* But Ik-su pretended not to notice.

"You've seen the news, too, right? Maybe the reporter told you?"

"I wonder why I keep watching the news with my

라는 단서를 달아서 옮겨준 말도 새록새록 돋아났다. 아버지는 좀 어떠시냐고 안부도 묻지 않아서 너무 무관심하다고 나무랐더니, 물어보나마나 빤한 사정을 물어서 어디쓰느냐고 반문합디다. 그는 영호를 야단칠까 망설이다 문득 적반하장이란 말을 떠올렸다. 누가 누구를 야단치고 누가 누구를 원망한단 말인가. 그의 깊은 내면에서 용수철처럼 죄의식이 솟구쳤다. 즐거운 이야기를 나누다가도 흡사 발작을 일으킨 간질병 환자처럼 정신을 잃고 뻐드러지는 병신, 먹어도 먹어도 삭정이처럼 마르기만 하는 병신, 의사들이 병명도 병인도 밝혀내지 못하는 희귀한 병신. 이 병신의 유전자들 중에 몸을 말리는 것만 빼고 큰놈한테 물려줬겠지.

익수는 쿵쿵 가슴을 치고 싶다. 심장이 찢어지게 억울하다. 눈두덩이 뜨끔해온다. 영호가 녹음기 속의 테이프를 꺼내고 그 옆의 다른 것으로 갈아 끼운다. 그는 아버지 쪽으로 고개를 돌리지 않는다. 모름지기 그 동작뿐이다. 익수가 움푹 꺼진 눈을 손끝으로 문지르고 호흡을 가다듬으며 영호를 지켜본다. 녹음기의 세계에 갇힌 아들을 건드리고 싶지 않다. 그 안에도 간직할 만한 사연과 시간이 흐르고 있다면 엎드린 삶도 성립할 테지. 그 안에도 농밀

body like this." Yeong-ho had a sarcastic smile on his face, a smile that seemed to ask how anything in this world could possibly have meaning. Ik-su again pretended not to notice. *Perhaps I could change the mood by joking?* He became hopeful.

"Only those who have become famous know this, but you know, it's not easy to become famous. Didn't it take me over twenty-five years?"

"So your continual survival on the brink of death was rewarded. Even better, your whole family was on TV."

Ik-su couldn't think of anything to say in response to this rapid reply. Yeong-ho turned his face away. *Father, let go of your obsession with my lower body.* Ik-su felt as if he had heard his son say this. He wanted more of a conversation with his son. But his son blocked his ears with earphones attached to a portable cassette player.

*

As on the previous day, Ik-su and Yeong-ho spent the morning without much interaction. The father was engaged with idle thoughts, and his son with this cassette player. Father and son seemed to have

한 연애는 있을 테지. 언뜻 익수가 미소를 지었다. 뜻밖의 궁금증 탓이었다. 과연 저 녀석은 숫총각이었을까? 군복 입을 기회도 없었으니……. 아니지. 요즘 세태가 어떤데. 몇 번은 경험했겠지. 아니지. 없어야 해. 그게 좋아. 아버지는 애써 아들이 숫총각이기를 바랐다. 만약 그게 아니라면 그 기억에 목말라서 더 심하게 자학할 것 같았다.

익수는 영호의 수음과 거의 맞닥뜨린 적이 있었다. 아들의 고1 겨울방학. 어느 대낮에 망치 쓸 일이 생긴 그가 아랫방 문고리를 당겼다. 안에서 걸려 있었다. 몇 초 지나서 방문이 열렸다. 그 찰나에 아버지의 코를 공격한 냄새는 밤꽃 향기 같은 비린내였다. 탐스런 복숭아 빛깔의 두 볼과 어떤 그리움에 사무쳤던 눈빛도 그는 놓치지 않았다. 그러나 아버지는 코가 없고 눈이 없었다. 공구통에서 망치 꺼내주라. 그저 편안한 부탁이었다.

영호는 녹음기의 세계가 따분해졌을까. 이어폰을 귓구멍에 박은 채 연필깎이 칼로 손톱을 다듬고 있다. 디테일 처리에 몰두하는 조각가를 연상시키는 품이었다. 아버지 따위는 안중에도 없어 보였다. 익수가 눈을 부릅떴다. 더는 침묵을 견딜 수 없었다. 억지 쓰는 대화보다야 침묵이 수월하겠다던 생각을 휴지처럼 구겨버렸다. 아버지의 야

nothing else to do. It was past two P.M. The languid quietude of a midday fishing village filled their shabby room. Deciding that silence was easier than awkward conversation, Ik-su was comparing, in his mind, the son in front of him with the son who was once healthy.

Yeong-ho was a well-mannered and affable young man. After getting a job in the steel plant, he would often visit his parents, a bag with *soju* bottles and Korean-style bacon tucked under his arm. *Get drunk just a little, Father.* He knew how to behave like a caring friend to his father, who was skinny as a dried pollack. But how was he these days? He couldn't be any brusquer. He even avoided conversation. His good manners in the old days seemed to have developed so far that even his heart had turned to stone. This was his first visit in five months, but he didn't even ask about his family. Although his younger brother hadn't come home and hadn't called, he didn't care at all. When his parents expressed worries at the dinner table about Yeong-seop, who hadn't been home for four days, he gruffly retorted. *He must be staying with his friends.* He was scolding them for making a fuss about nothing.

왼 손이 아들의 두툼한 어깨를 툭 건드렸다. 영호가 칼을 방바닥에 내려놓고 이어폰 하나를 빼내더니 느긋하게 고개만 틀었다.

"뭘 그렇게 열심히 듣고 있나?"

"노래요."

익수의 상상은 빗나갔다. 설교도 강연도 아니었다.

"어떤 노랜데?"

"서태지와 아이들, 마이클 잭슨, 양희은의 '한계령'도 듣고, 어떤 때는 '철의 노동자'도 들어요."

"듣기 좋은 꽃노래도 한두 번이지, 그렇게 하루 종일 노래만 듣고 있으면 귀가 안 아프나?"

"발랄한 율동의 음악을 들으면서 그걸 신나는 기분으로 정신없이 따라가다 보면 어느 한 순간에 발가락이 꼼지락거리게 될지 혹시 압니까?"

영호가 빙긋이 웃고 시선을 녹음기로 옮겼다. 마치 달관의 경지를 교만스레 뻐기는 것 같은 그 웃음이, 익수는 여전히 징그러웠다.

"영호야 너."

영호가 다시 고개만 돌렸다. 왜요, 라는 반문을 눈에 달고 있었다.

66

Ik-su felt sad again about his heartlessness toward his own younger brother. He was reminded of Yeong-ho's words, which his wife had relayed after she visited Yeong-ho in the prayer house, saying he shouldn't feel sad about it. She said that when she scolded Yeong-ho for not asking after his father, he asked what use there was in asking a question whose answer was so obvious. He thought of scolding Yeong-ho, but then suddenly remembered the phrase, "wrongdoer's audacity." *Who's scolding whom and who's resenting whom?* A guilty feeling quickly jumped up from deep inside him like a coiled spring. An invalid who loses consciousness and collapses like an epilepsy patient having a fit in the middle of a pleasant conversation, an invalid who becomes thinner and thinner like a withered branch no matter how much he eats, a rare invalid, the name and cause of whose illness even doctors can't identify—must have transmitted the damaged genes of those illnesses to his son except for the gene that causes weight loss.

Ik-su felt like banging on his own chest. He felt so heartbreakingly mortified. His eyelids were beginning to feel prickly. Yeong-ho took out a cassette from the player, and placed anther next to it. He

"아니다. 그만두자."

익수가 손사래를 쳤다. 그때 텔레비전 앞의 옥색 전화통이 따르릉거렸다. 참으로 고마운 전화를 받으려고 그는 재바르게 몸을 놀렸다.

"김익수 씨, 아니, 김익수 병장 맞아요? 양놈들이 원더풀을 연발하게 만든 그 김 병장?"

익수는 귀를 의심했다. 목소리는 아주 낯선데 '원더풀'이 냉큼 박 대위를 끌어냈다.

"박문현 화학관님! 맹호!"

익수가 신병처럼 소리를 질렀다. 영호는 고개를 들지 않았다.

"이게 몇 년 만인가? 거의 30년은 됐구나. 그날 뉴스를 보고는 일본에 다녀오느라고 며칠 지각을 했는데, 방송국에 전화해서 자네 번호 알아냈어. 금세 내 이름도 대고, 자네 기억력은 정상이구나."

박 대위가 말을 쉬었다. 익수가 병사처럼 떠들었다.

"기억력 말고도 쓸 만한 데가 많습니다."

영호가 이어폰 하나를 빼고 아버지의 등을 훑어보았다. 여태 멀쩡한 기능을 자랑하는 익수의 보고가 이어졌다.

"어떤 때는 오줌발도 기차게 셉니다. 삶은 감자 하나는

didn't turn toward his father. He was simply moving mechanically. Ik-su was staring at Yeong-ho, rubbing he sunken eyes with his hand and trying to breathe evenly. He didn't want to bother his son, who was imprisoned in his own world of the cassette player. There could be a life lying face down, if it was filled with memorable stories and times. There could be a ripe love affair, too. Suddenly Ik-su smiled. All of a sudden, he became curious. *Was Yeong-ho still a virgin? He even didn't even have the chance to wear a military uniform... Perhaps not, given the way of the world these days. He probably slept with a girl a few times at least. No, I hope not. To have had no experience would be better.* Father hoped that his son was a virgin. It seemed that if he weren't, he would probably be thirstier for that memory and the torment would be harsher.

Once Ik-su almost walked in on Yeong-ho masturbating. One winter day, when his son was a freshman in high school, he pulled the iron-ring handle of the door to his children's room, looking for a hammer. The door was locked from the inside. It opened a few seconds later. Ik-su's nose was immediately assaulted by a fishy smell like the fragrance from a chestnut blossom. He didn't miss the peach-

용감하게 무찌를 자신이 있습니다."

영호가 빙긋이 웃고는 뺐던 이어폰을 다시 귓구멍에 박았다. 박 대위가 자기의 이력을 알렸다. 대령 예편, 현재 무역회사 임원. 그리고 차분히 말을 이었다.

"요새는 사이공이 아니고 호치민이지. 이번 가을에는 들어갈 거야. 도이모이라고, 개방으로 나온 거야. 미구에는 그렇게 자본주의 방식으로 나올 것을, 빌어먹을 우리는 뭣 때문에 그렇게 독한 가루약을 퍼부어대며 악을 썼는지 몰라. 김 병장."

"예에."

"역사라는 거, 멀쩡한 사람들을 실컷 잡아먹은 다음에야 어느 순간에 정신을 차리고 바른길로 가는 괴물이야."

박 대위가 또 말을 쉬었다. 익수도 잠자코 있었다.

"이 사람아, 눈물이 나오네. 왜 뒤늦게 자네까지 잡아먹으려고 하나. 이 사람아, 자네 몰골이 그게 뭔가 말이야."

심호흡으로 눈물을 막아낸 익수가 박 대위의 상태를 염려했다. 자네 솜씨나 칭찬하고 명령이나 했으니 무슨 후유증이 생기겠느냐고 반문한 그가 불원간 자네를 만나러 가겠다고 했다. 익수는 일부러 씩씩하게 나갔다.

"기다리겠습니다. 그날은 이 멋진 남편이 일급 해녀로

colored cheeks and the light in his son's eyes, sparked by a certain longing. But he pretended not to have eyes or nose. *Please give me the hammer from the toolbox!* He asked gently.

Perhaps because he grew bored in the world of the cassette player, Yeong-ho was trimming his fingernails with a penknife, earphones still stuck in his ears. He reminded Ik-su of a sculptor absorbed in the detail of his work. He didn't seem to notice his father at all. Ik-su glared at him. He couldn't stand this silence any longer. He tossed away his previous thought—that silence would be better than awkward conversation—like a piece of crumpled tissue paper. He lightly touched his son's muscular shoulder with his scrawny hand. Putting the knife down on the floor and taking an earphone out of his ear, Yeong-ho slowly turned his head.

"What are you listening to so intently?"

"A song."

Ik-su's guess had been off the mark. He thought it would be a sermon or lecture.

"What song?"

"Seo Tae-ji and Kids, Michael Jackson, and sometimes '*Hangyeryeong*' by Yang Hui-eun and other

키운 아내에게 우리 앞바다에서 제일 좋은 전복을 따오게
하겠습니다."

"이 사람, 김 병장. 잘 버텨야 해. 내가 전복 얻어먹고
가을에 베트남 데려갈 거니까 무조건 버텨야 해. 그 동네
의 밀림들은 어떨까? 우리 둘이서 같이 확인해 보세. 이건
상관의 약속이고 명령이야."

박 대위가 전화를 끊었다. 익수가 송수화기를 내려놓았
다. 영호는 무덤덤한 표정으로 무언가를 듣고 있었다.

*

익수는 호리호리한 기자가 취재 기념품처럼 선물한 잡
지를 뒤적이고 있었다. 이미 정독했어도 또 고엽제 특집
에 손이 갔다. 그는 미국에서 베트남전쟁의 고엽제 후유
증 환자를 '느린 탄환(Slow Bullets)'이라 부르는 것에 깜짝
놀랐다. '서서히 그러나 마침내 심장에 박히는 총알. 아주
서서히 죽이는 살인, 슬로우 불릿.' 귀신같은 별명이어서
박수를 치고 싶었다. 선생님은 하필 베트남전쟁에서 고엽
제를 가장 대량으로 살포했던 시기에 화학작전을 했던 건
데, 여기를 읽어보세요. 그는 기자가 손톱으로 밑줄 친 곳

times '*Steel Workers.*'"

"I guess they're good songs, but don't you get tired listening to them all day long?"

"Who knows? If I keep devoting myself to listening to rhythmical music, I might find my toes moving a tiny bit, all of a sudden." Smiling sardonically, Yeong-ho glanced toward the cassette player. Ik-su found his smile, which seemed arrogantly to boast of having attained sage-like wisdom, creepy.

"Yeong-ho, hey!"

Yeong-ho turned his head again, asking with his eyes, *why?*

"No, forget it!" Ik-su waved his hand. At that very moment, the light blue phone by the TV set rang. Ik-su jumped to answer this most welcome call.

"Mr. Kim Ik-su, no, Sgt. Kim Ik-su, right? The Sgt. Kim who kept making the Yankees say 'wonderful'?"

Ik-su couldn't believe his ears. Although he didn't recognize the voice, the 'wonderful' immediately brought to mind Capt. Bak.

"Capt. Bak of the chemical division! Maengho!" Ik-su cried like a new recruit. Yeong-ho didn't raise his head.

"How long has it been? Almost thirty years. I'm

을 거듭 읽어보았다.

특집기사는 익수에게 여러 가지 새로운 정보를 알려줬다. 미군은 1967년부터 1971년까지 15종류의 고엽제를 베트남의 산림지대와 논 170만 헥타르에 살포했다. 익수가 화학작전에 동참하고 있던 1967년에 최대량을 퍼부었다. 미국에선 벌써 1979년부터 베트남전쟁 고엽제 후유증 환자들이 사회문제로 대두했다. 1983년에는 1만 2천여 명이 '베트남 재해군인 오렌지 희생자회'란 단체를 만들고 사회운동을 시작했다. 고엽제 피해자들이 고엽제에 다이옥신을 사용한 다우케미컬사 등 7개 제조회사를 상대로 400억 달러의 손해배상 청구소송을 제기했다. 1984년 5월 8일 브루클린 연방법원에서 재판이 열리기 몇 시간 전에 피고 측이 1억 8천만 달러의 기금을 제공하겠다고 한 협상안에 원고 측이 전격 합의함으로써 재판이 무산되었다.

400억과 1억 8천만. 익수는 그 엄청난 차액 때문에 청구소송이 아니라 소꿉장난이었나 하는 야릇한 의구심이 생겼다. 그러나 그것을 중요하게 여기진 않았다. 미국은 오래 전부터 베트남전쟁 고엽제 후유증 환자들이 사회적 이슈로 대두했고, 그 힘이 막강한 단체까지 조직했다는 사실에서 격려 같은 힘을 얻었다. 뚱뚱한 의사는 익수에

calling belatedly because I had to go to Japan right after I saw the news. I called the broadcasting station to get your phone number. You remembered my name right away. Your memory is still fine!"

Capt. Bak paused. Ik-su was chattering like a soldier. "I have many other useful things, not just my memory."

Taking out one of his earphones, Yeong-ho looked his father up and down. Ik-su continued boasting about his normal functions: "Sometimes my urine stream is amazingly powerful. I'm confident that I could bravely demolish a boiled potato."

After tossing his father a smile, Yeong-ho plugged the earphone back into his ear. Capt. Bak told Ik-su about his career. *Discharged at the rank of colonel, currently an executive at a trading company,* and he continued, "These days they call Saigon Ho Chi Minh City. I'm going there this fall. They adopted Doi Moi, an open-door policy. They would have adopted the capitalist way in the end. Goddamit! I wonder why we had to make such a fuss, pouring such strong poisons onto their land. Sgt. Kim!"

"Yes."

"So-called history—that's a monster that wakes up and goes in the right direction only after devouring

게 미국 고엽제 단체가 왜 '오렌지'란 이름을 붙였겠느냐고 물었다. 그는 쉽게 추측할 수 있었다. 술통처럼 생긴 낙엽살초제 통에 오렌지색 띠가 칠해져 있어서 그럴 거라고 했다. 의사가 영어로는 고엽제를 '에이전트오렌지'라 불렀다며 고개를 끄덕였다.

이제 익수는 면박 놓을 생각도 정리했다. 호리호리한 기자는, 한국의 형편상 정부가 주도적으로 나서지는 못하겠지만 우리나라에서도 베트남전 고엽제 상해자회 같은 조직이 더 단단해져야 하고 한국변호사협회 등이 도와서 미국 고엽제 제조회사들과 법적 소송도 벌여야 한다고 주장했다. 지금 그 말을 한다면, 익수는 왜 우리나라 언론은 미국 언론에 비해 뒷북을 쳐도 너무 늦게 치느냐고 따질 것이었다.

특집기사는 베트남의 고엽제 오염지역에서 태어난 기형 2세들에 대한 외신도 손바닥 크기의 박스에 담고 있었다. 익수가 흠칫했다. 퍼뜩 깨우친 일이 머리를 때린 것이었다. 박스의 외신은 반드시 숨겨야 하는 내용이었다. 영호가 집에 오기 전에는 독자의 가슴을 쓰리게 하는 사연이었지만 영호가 집에 있으니 또 다른 차원의 심각한 문제였다. 그 안에는 '하반신 마비'란 용어가 섞여 있는 것

many innocent people." Capt. Bak paused again. Ik-su remained silent as well.

"Hey, you, I can't help my tears. Why is it trying to devour you this belatedly? Geez, how could your body become like that?"

Ik-su could only keep from crying by taking a deep breath and asking after Bak's health. After asking what aftereffects could be experienced by someone who simply praised Ik-su's skills and ordered him about, Capt. Bak said he would visit Ik-su soon. Ik-su answered forcefully, on purpose, "I'll look forward to your visit. I'll ask my wife whom I, this wonderful husband, taught to become a first-rate diver to pick the best abalone in the sea by our village."

"Hey, Sgt. Kim, you have to stand your ground. I'll be treated with abalone and take you to Vietnam this fall. How are the forests there? Let's check it out together. This is my promise and order as your superior."

Capt. Bak hung up. Ik-su put down the receiver. Expressionless, Yeong-ho kept listening to something.

이다. 이걸 영호가 읽었다면, 아이쿠, 이제야 생각하다니……. 익수는 손에 든 잡지가 자신의 엄청난 범죄에 대한 결정적 단서 같았다. 어서 치워야 했다. 우선 급한 대로 잡지를 방구석으로 밀쳐버렸다.

"아버지."

영호가 불렀다. 익수는 당황했다. '하반신 마비'를 들킨 것 같았다.

"죄송해요."

영호가 손으로 엉덩이를 툭툭 건드렸다.

"이놈의 자식, 뭐가 죄송해!"

익수는 한숨을 돌린다는 것이 오히려 소리를 지르고 말았다. 하지만 아들은 엉덩이의 손을 거두어 정확히 이어폰을 집고 있었다.

쪽마루에 놓아둔 관장 도구. 통에는 비눗물이 충분히 들어 있다. 통 밑바닥의 한복판에 꽂힌 빨간 비닐호스는 가지런히 똬리를 틀고 있다. 변기통도 깨끗하다. 따로 더 손볼 것이 없었다.

익수는 통을 벽에 걸어놓은 뒤 영호의 인조견 잠옷과 사각팬티를 함께 발목으로 끌어내린다. 누르께한 알궁덩이가 드러나자 고약한 구란내가 코를 찌른다. 팬티에 변

*

Ik-su was flipping through the magazine the slender reporter had left, like a souvenir, after the interview. Although he had already perused the feature articles about defoliants, he found himself reading the same pages again. He was surprised to find that Americans called the suffering from the aftereffects of defoliants "Slow Bullets." A bullet that slowly but surely penetrates a patient's heart, a very slow murder, a slow bullet... The name was so exquisite that he wanted to applaud. *You have engaged in chemical operations during the time when Americans sprayed the most defoliants during the Vietnam War. Read here.* He read the part again and again that the reporter had underlined with his fingernail.

Ik-su acquired various pieces of new information from the special feature articles. From 1967 to 1971, U.S. army sprayed, in total, fifteen kinds of defoliants over 1.7 million hectares of mountains and rice paddies in Vietnam. They sprayed the biggest quantity in 1967, when Ik-su was participating in chemical warfare. In America, patients suffering the aftereffects of defoliants became a social issue in 1979. About twelve thousand people organized the

이 묻어 있다. 아버지가 아들의 허물 같은 옷을 벗겨서 쪽마루에 던져놓는다. 실낱 하나 안 붙은 영호의 다리가 퉁퉁하다. 하지만 어쩐지 바람 든 무 같다. 익수는 묵묵하다. 엎드린 영호는 자신의 다리와 항문이 자신과는 무관한 물체인 것처럼 그저 녹음기의 세계에 몰두하는 자세다. 아들의 오른 다리를 뛰려는 개구리 다리처럼 접은 아버지가 그 무릎 밑에다 베개를 받친다. 다음엔 일어서서 비닐호스의 끄트머리 부위에다 글리세린을 바른다. 이제 그것을 넣을 차례다. 아버지는 다시 앉아서 왼손의 엄지와 식지로 비닐호스의 한 지점을 야무지게 눌러 비눗물의 흐름을 차단하고 오른손으로 그 끄트머리를 아들의 항문 속에 꽂는다. 발기한 성기만큼은 쑤셔 넣어야 한다.

익수는 비닐호스의 한 지점을 눌렀다 폈다 되풀이하면서 비눗물이 들어가는 속도를 조절한다. 쪽마루의 팬티에는 어느새 파리들이 까맣게 엉겨 붙었다. 그는 짧은 곁눈질로 미물들의 왕성한 생명력을 보았다. 조금은 부러운 느낌이 일었다. 느긋하게 담배 한 대를 피울 만한 시간이 지나갔다. 통이 텅 비었다. 그가 비닐호스의 끄트머리를 빼내고 급히 수건을 뭉쳐 아들의 항문을 틀어막았다.

"아버지, 월남전 얘기나 해주세요."

Vietnam Veterans Agent Orange Victims, Inc. in 1983, launching a movement. The victims filed a forty-billion-dollar suit against seven manufacturers that used dioxin in defoliants, including Dow Chemical. There was no trial, because the plaintiffs accepted the defendants' offer of 180 million dollars only a few hours before the trial was to begin, on May 8th, 1984.

Forty billion and 180 million—because of the huge difference in those numbers, Ik-su couldn't help wondering whether this was a law real suit or a game, although that might sound weird. But that didn't matter to Ik-su. He felt encouraged that the aftereffects of defoliants had been a social issue for a long time and that the sufferers had even created a powerful organization. The chubby doctor asked Ik-su if he knew why the American organization included the word "orange" in its name. Ik-su guessed easily. He said it was probably because of the orange band painted around the defoliant containers that made them look like wine barrels. The doctor nodded and said that was why they called the defoliants Agent Orange.

Ik-su knew what he wanted to say next time to the reporter, who said that although the Korean

익수는 귀를 의심할 지경이었다. 아들과 대화를 나누고 싶다는 아버지의 마음이 비로소 아들의 항문을 통해 그 마음에 닿은 것 같았다.

"어떤 거?"

"재미있는 거요."

"고엽제는 재미없는데."

"그건 나도 싫고요. 뭐 신났던 일 없었어요?"

익수는 영호가 짓궂게 군다는 것을 알아차렸다. 아버지는 베트남에서 여자를 강제로 건드린 경험이 없나요. 이딴 소리 같았다. 하지만 그는 왼손으로 변기통을 집어다가 항문을 틀어막은 오른손 밑에 받치고 딴청을 부렸다.

"화염방사기 말이야. 그것 참 무섭대. 작전을 하다가 한번은 무논 논둑 밑에 대롱을 물고 물속에 숨어 있는 베트콩을 잡았어. 쪼그맣고 까만 놈이었는데, 그놈한테서 정보를 빼내자니 당장 손쉬운 방법은 고문밖에 더 있었겠나? 베트콩, 독하더라. 때리고 워커발로 걷어차도 절대 안 부는 거야. 자기들끼리는 해방전선 전사라 했는데, 정말 베트콩은 독종콩이더라. 삼십 분이나 짓이겼는데 입에서 나오는 소리가 그저 '꽁비야' 이 한마디뿐이라. 우리말로 '모른다'는 뜻인데, 실컷 두들겨 패고 기껏 얻어낸 소득

government wouldn't initiate the fight because of various circumstances, the Korean Association of Patients Suffering from the Aftereffects of Defoliants during the Vietnam War should become more powerful and file a suit against the American defoliant manufacturers, assisted by the Korean Bar Association. If the reporter said this again, Ik-su was going to ask him why the Korean media was so far behind the American media in reporting on this topic.

The feature articles included a palm-sized insert about the deformed babies born in the areas contaminated with defoliants during the Vietnam War, quoting overseas news. Ik-su shrank. He suddenly realized that he should keep this hidden. Before Yeong-ho visited, it was simply a heartbreaking article, but now it posed a problem, and a rather serious one. The article mentioned "waist-down paralysis." *What if Yeong-ho read this? Goodness, how come I didn't think of this before!* Ik-su felt as if he were holding a crucial piece of self-incriminating evidence in his hand. He had to get rid of it right away. He just randomly shoved it into a distant corner.

"Father!" called Yeong-ho. Ik-su was embarrassed.

이 '꽁비야'밖에 없었던 거지. 그래서 내가 나섰다. 이십 미터쯤 전방의 물속에다 놈을 세워놓고 화염방사기를 당겼지. 화염방사기는 9초 만에 다 나가는데 방아쇠를 살짝 당겼다가 놓으면 몇 번 나눠서 발사할 수 있다. 발가벗겨 놓은 독종콩 양옆에다 한 방씩 놓았더니 단 두 방 만에 항복을 하더라. 화염방사기는 그 불똥이 고무처럼 엉겨서 물 위에서도 탄단 말이야. 그게 만약 사람 몸에 붙으면 어떻게 되겠나? 그래서 베트콩 2명을 사살하고 3명을 생포하는 전과를 올리게 됐지."

해골 같은 얼굴에 웃음꽃마저 피어났다. 어린 아들을 데리고 무용담을 자랑하는 아버지 같았다. 내친 김에 그는 '감자캐기'도 들고 나왔다.

"그곳은 평야인데 늪이 많은 지역이었다. 중대와 대대 사이에 도로가 있고, 그 도로를 보호하기 위해 도로 매복을 나간다. 철수 시간에는 스리쿼터가 매복조를 태우러 나온다. 그날은 반환점 바로 앞이었다. 베트콩들이 지뢰를 인계철선에 연결해서 도로에 파묻어 놓고는 인근 감자 밭에 숨어 있었던 거야."

"트럭이 통째로 날아갔겠네요."

영호는 전쟁 영화의 한 장면을 지켜보듯 무덤덤했다.

He felt as if "waist-down paralysis" had been overheard.

"I'm sorry."

Yeong-ho patted his own butt.

Relieved, Ik-su ended up yelling, "Hey, what's there to be sorry about?" But his son stopped patting his butt and went straight back to his earphones.

There was a kit for an enema on the narrow veranda. There was enough soapy water in the syringe. A red hose was evenly coiled, connected to the syringe. The bedpan was clean, too. There was nothing more Ik-su had to do to get things ready.

After hanging the syringe on the wall, Ik-su pulled Yeong-ho's rayon pajama bottom as well as his shorts down to his ankles. A yellowish, naked butt appeared and an offensive smell greeted Ik-su's nose. Yeong-ho had soiled his shorts. Ik-su took off his son's fetid clothes and threw them onto the narrow veranda. Yeong-ho's naked legs were plump. But somehow they looked like spongy radishes. Ik-su was calm and quiet. Lying face down, Yeong-ho was absorbed in the world of the cassette player as if his own legs and anus had nothing to do with him. Folding his son's right leg like a frog's that was

"3명이나 전사했다. 부상자는 더 많았고. 그래서 '감자 캐기'라는 보복 작전이 있게 됐다. 그러나 작전은 신사적으로 시작됐다고 생각한다."

문득 익수가 어떤 증언대에 앉은 사람처럼 태도를 고쳤다. 영호는 무덤덤한 표정 그대로였다.

중대는 문제의 마을을 미리 포위하고 촌장에게 아침 10시까지 정해준 통로를 따라 일단 마을을 소개하라고 통보했다. 신분증 지참은 목숨과 같다는 말도 강조했다. 소개 시간은 30분 미만이었다. 신분증 없는 아낙들이 섞여 있었으나 우선 촌장의 보증에 따라 통과를 시켰다. 수색조가 마을로 들어갔다. 5분도 안 돼서 의심스런 지형지물을 발견했다. 포대와 바구니로 위장한 땅굴 입구 같았다. 중사가 상병에게 신호를 보냈다. 위협 사격에 M16 소총의 탄창 한 개를 소모했다. 그러나 안에서는 잠잠했다. 총알만 버린 격이었다. 중사가 고개를 갸웃거렸다. 그냥 까발리기에는 아무래도 수상쩍은 모양이었다. 중사가 김익수 병장에게 손짓을 보냈다. 그는 지체 없이 화염방사기를 정조준하고 한 방 먹어 보라고 외치듯 방아쇠를 당겼다. 무서운 불길이 땅 속의 어디로 달려간 것일까. 금세 두 젊은 사내가 비명을 지르며 밖으로 튀어나왔다.

about to jump, Ik-su put a pillow under his knee to support it. Then he stood up and applied some glycerin to the tip of the plastic hose. The next step was inserting it. Sitting down again, he inserted the tip of the hose into his son's anus with his right hand while stopping the soapy water from flowing down by pinching the hose hard with his left thumb and index finger. It had to go into the anus as long as the length of an erect penis.

By squeezing and releasing a spot on the plastic hose, Ik-su controlled the speed of the soapy water's flow. Flies were already swarming all over the shorts on the veranda. He stole a glance at them, observing the vitality of those tiny creatures. He felt somewhat envious. The time it would take to smoke a cigarette passed. The syringe was empty. After taking out the tip of the plastic hose, he hurriedly stuffed his son's anus with a balled-up towel.

"Father, tell me about the Vietnam War."

Ik-su couldn't believe his ears. It seemed that his wish to have a conversation with his son had finally reached Yeong-ho, through his anus.

"What kind of story?"

"Something interesting."

"고등학생이나 됐는지. 앳된 얼굴이었다. 몸에 불이 붙어 있었다. 그 순간에는 솔직히 나도 그걸 꺼줄 생각을 못했다. 또 그럴 사이도 없었다. 누군가 그대로 갈겨버렸던 거야. 숨어 있었으니 베트콩이 틀림없다고 생각한 거였고, 수류탄을 던질지도 모른다는 겁을 먹었고, 특히 중대 전우들이 죽고 다쳤으니 적개심과 복수심에 불타고 있었던 거지. 나중에 촌장은 항의했다. 신분증이 없어서 숨겨 났던 거라고. 신분증이 없으면 지정된 통로로 나와 봤자 청년인데 무사했겠느냐고. 그러나 중사는 총을 보여주며 그것은 말짱 개수작이라고 윽박질렀다. 베트콩 총은 중사의 손에 딱 한 자루 있었다. 두 청년의 것이었는지, 다른 누구의 것이었는지. 나는 모른다. 촌장의 말이 맞으면 두 양민을 학살한 거고, 그게 거짓말이면 두 베트콩을 잡은 거고…… 그런 식의 전쟁이 계속됐던 거다."

익수는 불붙은 몸으로 비명을 지르다 푹 꼬꾸라지는 두 청년의 처참한 최후를 먼 화면처럼 보고 있었다. 그런데 영호가 뚱딴지같은 문제를 냈다.

"아버지, 사마귀를 한자로 뭐라고 하는 줄 알아요?"

숨결이 거칠어진 익수가 눈을 껌벅거렸다.

"모르겠는데."

"Defoliants aren't fun."

"I don't want to hear about that either. Don't you have any exciting stories?"

Ik-su realized that Yeong-ho was being mischievous. He seemed to be asking, *haven't you raped a Vietnamese girl?* But bringing the bedpan close with his left hand and putting it under his right hand, which was stopping up his son's anus, he pretended he hadn't noticed.

"You know, the flamethrower, that thing was really scary. During an operation, we once found a Viet Cong hiding under the footpath between rice paddies, holding a straw in his mouth. A very dark-skinned, smallish guy. We wanted to get information from him, and what would have been easier than torture? The Viet Cong—they were really strong. He didn't say a word even after we beat him and kicked him with our boots. I heard they were calling themselves freedom fighters. The Viet Cong were truly tough Congs. After a thirty-minute thrashing, the only thing that came out of his mouth was 'kong biya.' It means 'I don't know.' So the only thing we got after beating him to a pulp was 'kong biya.' Then I took charge. After standing him up naked in the water twenty meters away, I pulled the

"당랑(螳螂)이라 합니다."

"당랑이라. 당랑, 이렇게 불러보니 사마귀 맛은 없어지고 점잖은 군자 맛이다."

"옛날 중국의 성현 장자(莊子)라고 들어보셨지요?"

"노자와 장자, 그 이름은 안다."

"『장자』라는 책에 이런 얘기가 나옵니다. 사마귀가 감히 수레를 막아서려고 버팁니다. 그러면 그 사마귀는 어떻게 되겠습니까?"

아들의 속셈이 뭔지 몰라도 아버지는 아들의 유식한 말에 솔깃해진다. 무엇보다도 대화 자체가 즐겁다.

"십중팔구는 수레에 깔려 죽겠지."

"맞습니다. 그래서 아예 상대도 안 되는 놈이 강적에게 덤비는 격을 당랑거철(螳螂拒轍)이라 합니다. 사마귀가 감히 수레를 막으려고 덤비다니 그게 보통 웃기는 일입니까? 돈키호테의 시조 같은 놈인지도 모르지요."

"정말로 당돌한 사마귀구나."

영호가 잠시 말을 쉬었다.

"아버지나 저나 당랑거철은 되지 맙시다."

"우리가 왜 당돌한 사마귀 짓을 하나. 그럴 힘도 없는 사람들인데."

trigger of the flamethrower. It empties in nine seconds, but you can shoot many times if you keep slightly pulling and letting go. After I aimed shots to the left and right of that tough Cong, he yielded. Flames from a flamethrower keep burning even in water, because they congeal like rubber. What would happen if those flames stuck to a person's body? As a result, we killed two Viet Cong and captured three."

A smile appeared on his skeletal face. He looked like a father proudly telling his young son tales of bravery. While he was at it, he told him the story of 'digging up potatoes.'

"It happened in a swampy field. There was a road between our company and the rest of the battalion, and we had to go out on an ambush to protect that road. When the ambush team withdrew, a Three-quarter truck drove in to give the team a lift. That day the Viet Cong had buried a landmine right at the turn, rigged with a tripwire, and it was waiting for us, hidden in the nearby potato field."

"The truck must have blown up completely."

Yeong-ho was cool and calm as if watching a scene in a movie.

"Three people died. More were injured. We car-

말뜻을 모르는 체하는 아버지의 가슴속으로 서늘한 한
기가 끼쳐들고 있었다. 죽음이 우리 앞의 수레 아닙니까.
이 말까지 아들은 차마 뱉지 못했다.

　"봄날에 장자를 열심히 읽었습니다."

　"기도는 안 하고? 운전사는 기도를 열심히 했다고 하던
데?"

　"그게 그거지요 뭐."

　"시간을 허비하지 않고 공부를 열심히 했다니 반갑다."

　영호가 망설이다 말을 이었다.

　"장자의 아내가 죽었을 때 혜자란 사람이 문상을 갔더
니 장자는 다리를 뻗치고 항아리를 두들기며 노래를 부르
고 있었다고 합니다."

　"그것 참 희한한 사람이네. 아내가 죽었는데, 너무 심하
잖아?"

　"혜자도 그런 힐난을 했습니다. 그러자 장자는 아내의
임종을 보고 자기도 처음에는 슬퍼했다고 합니다. 그런데
근본을 생각한 뒤에는 달라졌다는 겁니다. 생도 형체도
본래 없는 것이다, 이것이 장자의 깨달음입니다. 생과 사,
형체와 기가 모두 천지라는 큰집에 안식하면서 그 변화라
는 것이 마치 춘하추동 사시가 왔다가 가고 갔다가 다시

ried out a retaliation operation called 'digging up potatoes.' I think the operation started out in an honorable way."

Suddenly, Ik-su straightened his posture like someone sitting in the witness stand. Yeong-ho's expression didn't change.

Ik-su's company surrounded the village in question and ordered the village chief to evacuate everyone by 10 A.M. along a route designated by the company. They emphasized that villagers should cling to their IDs like life itself. They were given less than thirty minutes to evacuate. Some women didn't have their IDs, but they were allowed to pass, vouched for by the village chief. A search team entered the village. Within five minutes, they found something suspicious. Hidden behind sacks and baskets, which were being used for camouflage was the entrance of what seemed to be a dugout. The sergeant in charge motioned to a private first class. He emptied an M16 rifle magazine, firing warning shots. But there was no movement inside the dugout. It seemed a waste of bullets. The sergeant was tilting his head. He didn't seem sure if it was safe to enter the dugout. He motioned to Private First Class Kim Ik-su, who immediately aimed the

오듯이 무한히 순환하는 원리와 같다는 겁니다."

익수는 아들이 못마땅해도 잠자코 있었다.

"장자가 초나라에 가는 도중에 해골을 만나 말채찍으로 탁 치고 나서 이런 소리를 지껄인 적이 있습니다. 너는 욕망을 탐한 나머지 이 모양이 되었느냐, 전쟁에서 목이 베어졌느냐, 불선한 일을 저질러서 혈육에게 욕을 끼칠까 봐 이 모양이 되었느냐, 굶주리는 환난을 당했느냐, 아니면 수명이 그뿐이었느냐. 그러고는 그 해골을 베고 잠을 잤더니 꿈에 해골이 나타나서 너의 말은 모두 인생의 걱정이고 죽음의 세상에는 그따위 귀찮은 일이 없다고 하더랍니다. 그래서 장자가, 내가 염라대왕을 시켜 그대를 다시 온전한 사람으로 살려줄 테니 환생하겠느냐고 물었더니, 해골이 눈썹을 찌푸리고 수심에 싸여서 하는 말이, 내가 이 좋은 세상을 버리고 미쳤다고 인간의 고생을 다시 하겠느냐고 화를 내더랍니다. 아버지, 이게 다."

"됐다. 그만해라."

익수가 차갑게 잘랐다. 하지만 영호는 턱 밑의 녹음기를 상대하는 그 자세로 말을 이었다.

"저는 아직 생사에 관하여 장자의 경지를 잘 모릅니다. 여러 번 읽어서 줄줄 외기는 하지만…… 아버지와 어머

flamethrower directly at the dugout and pulled the trigger as if shouting, *here we go*. Where did those fearsome flames go? Immediately, two young men came running out, screaming.

"They looked young, maybe high school students. Their bodies were in flames. Frankly, I didn't even think of putting out the fire. We didn't have time for that. Someone else shot them right away. In his mind, there was no doubt they were Viet Cong, given that they were hiding, so he was worried that they might throw grenades at any moment. And since his fellow soldiers died and were wounded, he must have been burning with hatred and a desire for revenge. The village chief protested later. He said he hid the boys because they didn't have IDs. He asked if they would have been fine without them, even if they evacuated through the pre-arranged passage. But the sergeant rebuked him, saying he was talking nonsense, and showed him the gun he was holding in his hand. I don't know if it belonged to the two young men or someone else. If the village chief was right, then we massacred two innocent civilians. If it was a lie, then we killed two Viet Cong... That was how things were."

Ik-su was staring at the terrible death of those two

니, 특히 아버지가 득도의 장애물입니다."

"그건 또 무슨 소리야?"

한식경을 잠잠하던 뒷산의 뻐꾸기가 막 목청을 가다듬고 있었다.

"그렇다는 겁니다. 저 뻐꾸기 소리가 당랑거철, 그 수레를 끄는 말의 목에 걸린 요령 소리 같은데요."

"요상한 소리 작작해라. 장자가 뭐라고 했든 그 해골이 뭐라고 했든 살아 있는 것만큼 확실한 것은 없다. 다 헛소리다."

그러나 영호가 엉뚱하게 나갔다.

"아버지, 우리를 다룬 그 뉴스 말입니다. 기분이 나쁘던데요."

익수는 또 끌려갔다.

"그건 나도 그랬다. 그래도 그 호리호리한 기자는 호감이 가더라. 나같은 처지에 있는 전우들을 도와보겠다고 나섰던데, 협조를 해줘야지. 모레쯤 한 번 더 올 거다. 그날 기자가 해준 얘기로는 우리나라 '고엽제 피해 신고 센터'에 현재 1천100여 명이 접수했는데, 그 중에 신체 마비 증상자만 해도 109명이나 된단다. 조만간 정부가 나서서 심사를 하게 되는데, 그때 가서 씨에스파우더 얘기는 꺼

young men, on fire and screaming and finally collapsing, as if watching a distant screen. Suddenly,
Yeong-ho asked him a farfetched question.

"Father, do you know what a wart's called in
Chinese?"

Panting a little, Ik-su blinked.

"No, I don't."

"It's tanglang."

"Tanglang, hmm, that sounds less like a wart, and
more like a dignified scholar."

"You've heard about Zhuangzi, the Chinese sage,
haven't you?"

"I've heard the names Lao Tzu and Zhuangzi."

"In a story from *Zhuangzi*, a wart dares to block a
wagon. What do you think will happen to the
wart?"

Although father wasn't sure why son was telling
him this story, he became curious about this intrigu-
ing puzzle. Above all, he was enjoying the conversation.

"Most likely, it would be squashed to death under
the wagon."

"That's right. So they call a weak person daring a
strong enemy 'Danglanggeocheol.' A wart daring to
block a wagon—isn't that ridiculous? That wart was

내지 말라는 충고도 해주더라. 복잡하게 만들지 말고 고엽제 얘기만 하라는 거지. 돈이나 몇 푼 얻자면 그러면 되겠지만, 나는 내 병인과 병명이라도 알아내는 게 소원이다. 그런데 말이다, 우리나라 고엽제 환자 2세 중에서 신체 마비 증상은 없다고 하더라."

"이제 다 된 거 같은데요."

영호가 아버지의 의도를 거절했다. 익수는 버텼다.

"조금 더 있어라. 깨끗하게 다 빼내야지. 우리 큰놈의 허리는 말이다, 내 생각에."

"아까부터 배꼽 밑이 꾸르륵거렸어요. 얘기느라고 더 기다렸는데, 다 됐어요. 지금부터는 시원한 기분으로 신나는 음악이나 들을게요."

"알았다, 임마."

익수가 변기통과 수건을 쪽마루에 내놓았다. 영호의 팬티에 붙은 까만 점들이 겁내는 시늉만 하고 다시 내려앉는다. 그 사이에 영호는 이어폰으로 두 귓구멍을 막는다. 방 안에는 뻐꾸기 울음소리가 쌓이고 있다. 뻐어꾸욱, 뻐어꾸욱, 뻐어꾸욱……. 불현듯 익수의 귀에 저승길 떠나는 고독한 혼백에게 바치는 목탁 소리처럼 들린다. 아들에게 사각팬티를 입혀주는 아버지가 두 손을 떨고 있다.

probably the forefather of Don Quixote."

"That's a really reckless wart."

Yeong-ho paused for a while.

"Father, let's not become Danglanggeocheol."

"Why would we act like a reckless wart? We don't have the power to do even that."

Pretending not to understand, Ik-su felt a chill in his heart. *Isn't death the wagon in front of us?* His son didn't dare spit that out.

"I enjoyed reading Zhuangzi in the spring."

"You weren't praying? The driver said you were praying devoutly."

"Reading and praying—they're all the same."

"I am glad to hear you haven't wasted your time and studied hard."

After pausing, Yeong-ho continued, "When Zhuangzi's wife died, someone named Hyeja made a condolence call and found Zhuangzi singing a song, beating a jar."

"What a weird guy! His wife died and he did that? That's too much!"

"Hyeja scolded him like that, too. Then Zhuangzi answered that he also felt really sad right after his wife's death. But he said he changed his mind after thinking about the fundamentals of the universe.

*

　영어를 몰라도 미군 교관에게 '원더풀'을 받은 익수는 며칠 뒤부터 화학무기를 만졌다. 씨에스파우더와 에이전트오렌지였다. 씨에스파우더를 파우더라 불렀다. 질식독가스라 부르지 않았다. 무시무시한 이름이 꺼림칙한 모양이었다. 에이전트오렌지를 오렌지라 부르지 않았다. 고엽제도 아니고 낙엽살초제라 불렀다. 만만한 이름으로 여긴 모양이었다. 그는 군수창고의 중사가 부르는 대로 불렀다.

　익수는 곧 작전에도 투입되었다. 박문현 대위가 무게 잡고 말한 대로 그게 한국군 최초인지 아닌지 몰라도 밀림의 상공으로 날아가는 헬기를 트럭보다 자주 탔다. 전투태세로 트럭을 타는 것은 보병의 작전을 지원하는 경우였다. 이때는 화염방사기를 맡았다.

　헬기에서 농약처럼 살포하는 씨에스파우더. 처음의 서너 달 동안에 익수는 그놈의 독가스를 껴안고 살아야 했다. 그놈을 옮겨 붓는 작업이 지옥이었다. 제조회사가 그놈을 출하할 때 헬기 배때기에 매다는 가정용 엘피지 가스통 같은 용기에다 담아줬다면 얼마나 좋았을까. 그놈을 석회나 담을 포대에 넣어서 팔아먹은 것이었다.

There was neither life nor matter originally—that's what Zhuangzi realized. Life and death, and matter and energy—all of them reside in the big house of the universe; transformation from one to the other is, in principle, like the eternal circulation of the four seasons."

Although Ik-su didn't like what his son was saying, he kept quietly listening.

"When Zhuangzi ran into a skeleton on his way to the country named Chu, he lashed it with his whip and asked, 'How did you become like this? Were you too greedy? Did you have your throat cut in war? Did you commit a wicked crime and kill yourself in order not to dishonor your family? Did you encounter famine? Or, did you live out your fated lifespan?' Then, he slept, using that skeleton as his pillow, and then the skeleton appeared in his dream and said, 'Your words are all about the worries of human lives, and there are no such worries to bother us in the world of death.' So Zhuangzi asked him if he'd like to come back to life if Zhuangzi could petition Yama on his behalf. The skeleton, frowning and with a worried expression, said, angrily, 'Do I seem crazy enough to leave this wonderful world to return to such a hard life in the human world?'

포대 속의 씨에스파우더를 가스통 속으로 옮겨 붓는 작업은 처음부터 끝까지 익수 단독으로 처리했다. 맨 먼저 나무를 이용해 판초우의 두 장으로 밀폐공간을 만들었다. 독가스가 바람에 흩날릴 위험을 예방하는 것이었다. 공정은 단순했다. 거의 턱까지 올라오는 가스통의 주둥이에다 깔때기를 꽂아놓고 포대 속의 그놈을 옮겨 붓는다. 그러나 밀가루보다 보드라운 분말 독가스는 손가락을 끼울 만한 구멍 속으로 술술 들어갈 수 없었다. 그가 쇠꼬챙이로 가스통의 협소한 구멍을 쉴 새 없이 쑤셔야 했다. 오른손 왼손 번갈아 쑤시기. 그것은 운동이라 여기면 그만이었다. 미칠 지경으로 몰아넣는 것은 더위였다. 늘 그랬지만 그의 육감에는 독가스가 아니라 더위가 판초우의의 밀폐공간을 폭파시킬 것 같았다.

미군 교관은 익수에게 밀폐공간에서 씨에스파우더를 취급할 때는 방독면, 우의, 장화, 장갑 등을 반드시 착용해야 한다고 가르쳤다. 그는 수칙대로 시작했다. 그러나 5분을 견딜 수 없었다. 몸이 삶기는 것 같았다. 더구나 가스통은 10개씩 20개씩 대기하고 있었다. 알몸도 쩌죽을 처지에서 영어의 수칙은 버려서 마땅한 수칙이었다. 군대는 요령이다. 이 진리의 신봉자가 될 수밖에 없었다. 그는 홀

Father, this is all..."

"That's all right. I get it," Ik-su cut him short coldly. But Yeong-ho continued, still looking as if he was calmly listening to the cassette player.

"I don't know very much about Zhuangzi's level of wisdom about life and death. I've read him so many times that I can recite his words... but father and mother, especially, you, Father, are the stumbling block to my attainment of Nirvana."

"What the heck are you talking about?"

The cuckoos that had been quiet for a while were beginning to clear their throats on the hill behind the house.

"I mean what I'm saying. Those cuckoo sounds seem like the bell on the neck of the horse pulling the wagon, the wagon of Danglanggeocheol."

"Stop talking nonsense. Whatever Zhuangzi said, whatever that skeleton said, there is nothing as sure as living. That's all nonsense."

But Yeong-ho abruptly changed the subject. "Father, that news program about us, I found it offensive."

Ik-su was being drawn in again. "I felt offended, too. Still, I liked that reporter. He's trying to help veterans like me. I'd like to help him. He's going to

홀 벗었다. 윗도리에는 러닝셔츠, 아랫도리에는 팬티와 장화만 남았다. 결코 벗지 못할 또 하나가 있었다. 방독면이었다. 머리가 삶은 돼지머리로 바뀌는 한이 있어도 그것만은 벗을 수가 없었다. 그것을 벗고 덤빈다면 당장 판초우의 안에서 질식할 것이었다. 하지만 작업할 때마다 방독면마저 벗고 싶은 유혹이 강렬했다. 다행히 그는 그것을 물리칠 부적 같은 주문을 욀 수 있었다. 한밑천 잡겠다고 남의 전쟁터에 왔는데 미쳤다고 독가스 옮겨 붓다가 죽어!

빨리 끝내는 것이 상책이란 일념에 매달린 익수가 30분 정도 작업에 열중하면 어느덧 발바닥이 질퍽질퍽했다. 온몸의 땀이 장화 속에 모인 것이었다. 하지만 땀은 아무런 문제도 아니었다. 샤워를 해주고 물을 실컷 마셔주면 그만이었다.

작업을 마친 익수는 곧장 샤워실로 달려갔다. 언제나 그랬다. 땀 때문에? 더위 때문에? 아니었다. 피부 때문이었다. 손등, 팔뚝, 목, 얼굴 등이 벌겋게 부어올랐다. 통증도 심했다. 수많은 침들이 한꺼번에 마구 쑤셔대는 것 같았다. 발가벗고 서서 찬물을 맞는 익수의 일은 하염없이 기다리는 것이었다. 한 시간이든 두 시간이든 부기가 가

come again the day after tomorrow. According to him, there are now 1,100 reported cases at the Victims of Defoliants Report Center. As many as one hundred and nine are suffering from paralysis. Pretty soon our government will investigate. He advised that I shouldn't even mention CS powder. I would do that, if I only wanted some money from them, but all I want is to know the cause and name of my illness. By the way, I heard that there weren't any cases of paralysis in the children of patients suffering the aftereffects of defoliants."

"I think I'm done." Yeong-ho ignored what his father was implying. Ik-su stood his ground.

"Wait a minute. Let's wait until all of it comes out. Regarding your back, I think..."

"It's been rumbling below my navel for a while. I waited because we were talking, but I think it's done. I'll listen to some exciting music now."

"OK, fine."

Ik-su took the bedpan and towel to the narrow veranda. The black dots covering Yeong-ho's shorts pretended that they were scared for a second, then landed right back on them. Meanwhile, Yeong-ho had blocked his ears again with his earphones. The cries of the cuckoos were piling up in the room.

라앉고 벌건 색깔이 스러질 때까지 기다려야 했다. 손은 금물이었다. 긁거나 문지르면 화상처럼 쓰라렸다. 피부가 정상으로 돌아온 다음 차례는 수건을 쓰는 것이 아니었다. 수건으로 닦을 수 없었다. 수건으로 배꼽 밑만 가리고 밖으로 나갔다. 발가벗은 그대로 통풍 좋은 나무 그늘에 들어가서 이십 분이든 삼십 분이든 서 있어야 했다. 나무 그늘 속에 서 있으면 약속처럼 신묘한 순간이 도래했다. 별안간 모든 통증이 사라지고 다시 몸이 성성해졌다. 번번이 그랬다. 고생은 길어야 두세 시간이었다.

익수가 나체로 나무 그늘 속에 서 있을 때는 장교나 하사관이 놀려 먹었다. 그들의 심심풀이 땅콩 같은 말은 나중에 하나로 통일되었다. 헤이 김 병장, 냄비도 없는 몸으로 또 스트립쇼를 하는 거야? 그때 익수는 '나 병장'으로도 통하고 있었다. '나체 병장'이란 뜻이었다. 가끔 깡통 맥주를 함께 마시는 졸병들도 익살스레 '나 병장님'이라 했다. 그는 고깝게 여기지 않았다. 저 친구들은 작전 나갔다가 언제 어디서 귀신이 되거나 병신이 될지 모르는데, 나는 발가벗고 팔자 좋게 나무 그늘에서 쉬지 않느냐. 이런 생각을 했던 것이다.

익수는 사나흘에 한 번씩 포대 속의 씨에스파우더를 가

Cuckoo, cuckoo, cuckoo... Suddenly, they sounded to Ik-su like the striking of a woodblock, sounds dedicated to a lonely soul on its way to the other world. Pushing his son's legs through a pair of shorts, Ik-su's hands were shaking.

*

Praised by the American instructors as "Wonderful!" even though he didn't know English, Ik-su began to handle chemical weapons a few days after his training course. The chemical weapons were CS powder and Agent Orange. CS powder was called simply "the Powder." They didn't call it asphyxiant gas. They probably wouldn't have felt comfortable calling it by that terrifying name. They didn't call Agent Orange "Orange." They didn't even call it defoliant, but herbicide, instead. They must have felt more comfortable calling it that. Ik-su used the names the sergeant used at the magazine.

Ik-su was soon sent into the field. Although he wasn't sure whether he was the first to do this, as Capt. Bak had solemnly declared, he was in a helicopter flying over thick forests more often than he was in the truck. He was in the combat truck when

스통에 옮겨 부었다. 그 작업을 넉 달쯤 계속했다. 그러니까 넉 달 동안을 사나흘에 한 번씩 판초우의 두 장으로 만든 밀폐공간에 갇혀 질식 독가스의 고문을 당한 것이었다.(익수는 호리호리한 기자에게 사진 석 장을 건네줬다. 비료 포대처럼 쌓은 씨에스파우더 포대들 앞에 홀로 쪼그려 앉은 김익수 병장, 헬기에서 농약처럼 씨에스파우더를 살포하는 장면, 그리고 헬기 안에 앉아 있는 건장한 모습의 박문현 대위와 김익수 병장.)

넉 달이 지나자 그놈의 독가스를 가스통으로 옮겨 붓는 작업이 없어졌다. 씨에스파우더 포대들을 차곡차곡 집어넣은 나무 박스를 헬기에 싣고 올라가 그것 자체를 공중에서 폭발시키면 되었다. 독가스를 더욱 무더기로 퍼붓는 짓이었지만 익수는 만세를 부르고 싶었다. 숙달된 솜씨로 폭파 장치만 다루면 그만이었다. 다만 코와 목은 고생이었다. 폭파 장치를 장착할 때 어쩔 수 없이 그놈에게 코를 박고 있으면 그놈이 방독면에 구멍을 뚫는지 목구멍이 화끈화끈 뜨거웠다.(익수는 호리호리한 기자에게 러닝셔츠 차림으로 그놈의 나무 박스 앞에 쪼그려 앉아 활짝 웃는 자신의 독사진을 보여주기만 했다. 그것은 한 장밖에 없었다.)

나무 박스 다음은 드럼통이었다. 씨에스파우더가 얼마

supporting infantry operations. In those cases, he was in charge of the flamethrower.

CS powder was sprayed like herbicide from the helicopter. For the first several months, Ik-su had to practically live in the stuff. He had to carry and pour it, and the work was hell. How nice it would have been if the manufacturer had shipped it in those containers hanging from the bottom of the helicopter, containers that looked like LPG canisters! Instead they sold the powder in sacks like those for lime.

Ik-su was the only person responsible for pouring CS powder out of the sacks and into those containers, like gas canisters, from start to finish. First he created an airtight space using trees and two raincoats. This was done to prevent the poisonous gas from being blown around by the wind. The process was simple. After sticking a funnel into the neck of a container so tall it almost came up to Ik-su's jaw, he poured the powder from the sack. But the poisonous powder, finer than flour, usually did not pour neatly into that tiny, finger-sized hole. Ik-su had to keep poking at the narrow hole with a skewer. He kept shifting this skewer from hand to hand, considering it exercise. But what was maddening was the

나 무서운 독가스인지 얇은 철판으로 만든 띠가 드럼통을 꽁꽁 묶고 있었다. 그러나 익수는 휘파람을 불었다. 방독면을 쓰면 코도 목도 아프지 않았다. 그는 드럼통도 나무 박스처럼 공중 폭발로 처리했다. 헬기 바닥에 깔아둔 도르래를 이용해 가볍게 드럼통을 투하할 수 있었다. 그의 주요 임무는 두 가지였다. 드럼통에 폭파 장치를 장착하는 것, 드럼통을 투하하는 것. 조종실의 뒤통수에 빨간불이 들어오면 준비를 하고, 파란불이 들어오면 핀을 뽑고 즉시 드럼통을 밖으로 밀어낸다. 투하와 거의 동시에 헬기는 급상승한다. 드럼통의 파편을 피하려는 것이다. 그의 손재주는 탁월했다. 투하한 드럼통은 하나도 말썽을 일으키지 않았다. 투하 3초 내지 4초 후에 틀림없이 자동으로 폭발했다. 조종사 옆에 앉은 화학관(주로 박문현 대위)의 역할은 따로 있었다. 고도와 풍향을 고려하는 투하 시각과 좌표를 결정했다. 날씨나 적의 저항 정도에 따라 작전을 취소하는 것도 그의 판단에 달려 있었다.

익수의 손을 거친 독가스는 밀림 지역에 쏟아졌다. K라는 밀림 지역을 A, B, C, D의 네 구역으로 나눈다고 하자. 아군이 A구역의 작전을 마치고 B구역으로 이동한다. 그러면 B구역에 있던 베트콩들이 안전해진 A구역으로 이동

heat. He always felt that the heat, not the poisonous gas, would cause an explosion in that airtight space made from raincoats.

The American instructor taught Ik-su that he had to always wear a gas mask, raincoat, boots, and gloves when handling CS powder. Ik-su started out faithfully following these instructions. But he couldn't last longer than five minutes in all that gear. His body seemed on the verge of boiling. Besides, more containers were waiting by the dozens. He had to dispense with the instructions written in English in heat so intense he thought he would die even if naked. *The military is all about discretion.* He had to become a believer in this dictum. He took off his clothes. He was wearing only an undershirt, shorts and boots. One thing he couldn't take off was the gas mask. He couldn't take it off even if his head would have turned into a boiled pig head on the spot. If he took it off, he would have been suffocated instantly in that airtight space. But he felt strongly tempted whenever he was working with the powder. Luckily he was able to recite a spell that served like an amulet, making him resist that temptation. *I got involved in a war of complete strangers to earn some money. I shouldn't*

할 가능성이 높다. 아군은 A구역을 아예 사람이 못 살게 만들고 싶다. 이때 A구역에 씨에스파우더를 눈처럼 살포한다. 낙엽살초제를 뿌리는 경우에는 당장의 적보다 미래의 적을 상대한다. 숲을 말리고 불을 질러서 사람도 짐승도 내쫓는 작전을 당일에 해치울 수는 없다. 보병의 작전이 불가능한 지역에도 그놈의 씨에스파우더와 낙엽살초제를 사정없이 퍼붓는다.

익수는 헬기 안에서 지상의 상황을 확인할 수 있었다. 무전 교신을 들어보면 효과가 만점이었다. 사람들이 정신없이 튀어나온다, 옷으로 입을 막고 꼬꾸라진다, 술 취한 것처럼 비틀비틀 헤매고 있다, 아기를 안은 여자 2명과 꼬마를 데린 여자 3명이 에이전트오렌지를 눈이라도 환영하듯이 두 팔을 벌려 맞고 있다. 재미난 놀이를 중계하는 것 같은 보고들이 왕왕거렸다.

씨에스파우더로 단련한 익수는 에이전트오렌지를 우습게 여겼다. 그에게는 질식독가스가 농약이라면 낙엽살초제는 비료에 불과했다. 실제로 그는 기지 주변의 풀숲을 제거하는 작업에서 낙엽살초제를 비료처럼 뿌리곤 했다. 기지 주변의 우거진 풀숲은 지휘관이나 병사들에게 두려운 지형지물이었다. 적이 숨어들거나 매복할 수 있기 때

be so crazy as to risk my life pouring poison gas!

After about thirty minutes of attentive work, only thinking the sooner he finished, the better, Ik-su would fine that his boots had become slushy inside. Sweat from his entire body was pooling in them. But it didn't seem that big a deal. He could simply take a shower later and drink a lot of water.

As soon as he finished work, Ik-su ran straight to the shower room, like always. Was it because of the sweating? Or, just the heat, generally? No, it was because of his skin. The backs of his hands, his arms, his neck, and his face were swollen and red. It was also very painful. It felt as if innumerable needles were randomly pricking his skin. Standing under the shower, naked, Ik-su waited patiently. He had to wait until the swelling subsided and the redness disappeared. This could take an hour or two. Touching was a taboo. If he happened to scratch or rub his skin, it felt as sore as a burn. Even after his skin became normal, he couldn't use a towel. He couldn't rub it over his skin. He held a towel under his navel and went out. He had to stand naked in well-ventilated shade, sometimes for ten minutes, and other times for twenty. While he was standing like that under a tree, a marvelous moment would

문이다. 한국의 야전에서 해온 버릇대로 낫이나 들고 설칠 수는 없었다. 좀 과장해서 말한다면, 베고 돌아서면 우거지는 풀숲이었다. 그래서 화학병이 조달해 온 미제(美製) 낙엽살초제는 당연히 인기가 높았다. 경계 병력을 포함해 흔히 소대 병력을 동원하는 기지 주변 풀숲 제거 작전에서 익수는 교관 노릇을 맡았다. 왼손은 낙엽살초제 가루를 듬뿍 담은 철모를 가슴에 안고, 오른손은 그것을 한 줌씩 집어 생명력이 왕성한 식물에게 비료처럼 뿌리는 시범을 보여주는 노릇이었다. 싱거운 졸병들은 박수를 쳤다. 제초 작업의 땀범벅을 면제시켜주는 해결사에게 바치는 감사의 뜻이었을 것이다.

*

    숙희는 저녁상에 전복죽을 올렸다. 아들을 위해 큰맘 먹고 손바닥만 한 전복 두 개를 돈과 바꾸지 않았다. 부부가 겸상으로 마주앉고, 영호는 휠체어를 타고 앉았다. 그의 밥상은 영섭의 의자였다. 익수가 아내에게 맛있다는 칭찬을 하고, 숙희는 남편에게 간이 알맞다고 했다. 그러나 영호는 동생의 의자 위에 놓인 사발을 관찰하듯 들여

arrive, like a promise fulfilled. Suddenly, all the pain disappeared and his body felt refreshed. That was always the case. The whole ordeal lasted two to three hours at most.

Commissioned and non-commissioned officers made fun of Ik-su while he was standing under the tree like that. Their silly jokes soon became predictable. *Hey, Sgt. Na! Are you doing a striptease without a pussy?* Ik-su was called Sgt. Na, an abbreviation of Sgt. Naked. Even his subordinates with whom he sometimes drank cans of beer also jokingly called him "Sir Sgt. Na." He didn't mind. *They could become ghosts or disabled at any moment out in the field, but I can rest under a tree shade, naked,* he thought.

Ik-su carried out the work of pouring CS powder every three or four days for four months. In other words, he was imprisoned in that airtight space made by two raincoats and tortured by asphyxiant gas every three to four days for four months. (Ik-su gave three photographs to the reporter: Sgt. Kim Ik-su squatting by himself in front of piles of CS powder sacks that looked like sacks of fertilizer; a helicopter spraying CS powder like herbicide; a robust looking Capt. Bak Mun-hyeon and Sgt. Kim Ik-su in

115

다보고 있었다. 몇 번인가 그 꼴을 곁눈질한 부부가 기어이 참견을 했다.

"뭐하고 있나?"

"어서 먹어라. 그만하면 먹기 좋게 식었다."

영호가 전복죽에게 탄식했다.

"이 귀한 음식이 아버지한테는 살이 안 되고 나한테는 똥만 되니."

"임마. 오늘 왜 그래? 낮에는 장자가 어떻고 해골이 어떻고 하면서 속을 뒤집어 놓더니. 내가 무식해서 못 알아들었지 싶나? 정말로 그럴래?"

"아버지는 많이 잡수세요."

"왜 이래 속을 뒤집나. 더 못 먹겠다!"

익수가 버럭 고함을 지르며 거칠게 숟가락을 놓았다.

"당신까지 왜 이래요?"

그러나 숙희는 아들을 째려보았다. 영호는 세상만사에 달관한 것 같은 그 웃음을 빙긋이 머금고 있었다.

"오냐 그래. 너 굶으면 몽땅 같이 굶자."

숙희가 숟가락을 놓고 매섭게 일어나서 영호의 사발을 밥상으로 옮겼다.

"방송이고 뭐고 다 치우고 내일 아침에 당장 기도원으

116

the helicopter.)

After four months, he no longer had to pour that poisonous gas. Instead he had to load wooden boxes filled with CS powder sacks onto the helicopter and then explode them in midair. Although this would spray even more poisonous gas all at once, Ik-su felt like cheering. All he had to do was attach an explosive device to the boxes. But his nose and throat suffered from this work, too. When his face was close to the box while attaching the explosive device, his throat was burning, perhaps because the gas was seeping through his gas mask. (Ik-su showed the reporter a photograph of himself in an undershirt, laughing heartily while squatting in front of the wooden boxes. That was his only copy.)

After the wooden boxes came the drums. One could judge how fearsome a poisonous gas CS powder was by the thin band of iron plate tightly circling each drum. But Ik-su was whistling. Inside his gas mask, he didn't feel any pain—not in his nose, or in his throat. He exploded the drums midair as he did the wooden boxes. He could lightly drop the drums using a pulley on the floor of the helicopter. There were two major tasks for him:

로 돌아가라. 말도 안 하고, 빙긋이 웃기나 하고, 밥도 먹는 둥 마는 둥 하고. 그럴 거면 오지 말지. 엄마 아버지 속 뒤집으러 왔나? 꼴도 보기 싫다. 엄마가 불쌍치도 않나!"

익수는 아들에게 모진 소리들을 사정없이 퍼부었다. 앙상한 가슴속에서 뭉클한 덩어리가 북받쳤다. 숨이 막혔다.

"당신 괜찮아요? 이러다가 또 큰일 납니다. 참으세요. 제발 고정하세요."

"더 말할 기운도 없다. 밥상 치워라. 눕고 싶다."

익수는 호흡이 곤란해서 헉헉거리고 있었다.

"호야, 왜 그래? 정말 속 썩일라고 왔나?"

"뻐꾸기 우는 소리 듣고 싶어서 왔다."

영호가 어머니를 쳐다보며 빙긋이 웃었다.

"그걸 말이라고 하나? 복음기도원에도 숲이 좋은데, 거기는 뻐꾸기도 없나?"

"엄마. 그만하자. 나도 눕혀주라. 자고 싶다."

숙희는 뺨을 갈기려 했다. 그러나 전화통이 따르릉 따르릉 말렸다.

"섭아. 어디야?"

익수와 영호의 시선이 송수화기로 쏠렸다.

"그래. 학교에 안 빠진 줄은 나도 안다. 내가 전화해서

attaching an explosive device to the drum and dropping the drum. When the red light behind the cockpit came on, he got ready. When the green light came on, he took out the safety pin and pushed the drum down immediately. As soon as the drum dropped, the helicopter soared up suddenly to avoid the drum fragments. Ik-su's skill was superb. No drum he dropped ever caused any trouble. This was impressive given that they automatically exploded three to four seconds after being dropped. The officer in charge of chemistry (mostly Capt. Bak Mun-hyeon), sitting next to the pilot, had a separate task. He decided on the time and coordinates for the drop, taking into account the height and wind direction. He could also cancel the operation, based on weather conditions or the level of enemy resistance.

Poisonous gas was poured onto the forests by Ik-su's hands. Let's suppose that we divide forest K into four sections, A, B, C, and D. After completing an operation in Section A, the military moves to Section B. Then, there is a strong possibility that the Viet Cong will move from Section B to Section A, which just became safer. So the military wants to make Section A uninhabitable. They spray CS pow-

알아 봤다. 섭아, 딴소리 그만하고 얼른 집에 들어와. 형
도 와 있다. 형 얼굴이라도 봐야지. 아버지가 화나서 내일
아침에 형을 돌려보내신단다. 약도 새로 사다 놨다. 어서
오너라. 아직 막차까지는 많이 남았잖아."

아침 7시 10분에 마을 정류장에서 버스를 타고 갔다가
저녁 7시쯤 버스를 내려 집으로 돌아오는 영섭. 비가 오나
눈이 오나 등교든 귀가든 지각 한 번 안 하던 모범생이 닷
새째 외박을 앞두고 처음 집으로 전화를 걸었다. 작은놈
의 말을 듣는 어머니의 눈가에 주름살이 깊어졌다.

"그 의사 말을 믿어라. 습진 연고만 발라왔지, 피부과
가서 진찰받은 적은 없잖아? 그게 왜 불치병이야? 습진이
아니고 백선이라 했잖아? 백선에 습진연고를 발라대면 덧
나기 쉽다고 했잖아? 그 의사 말이 맞잖아? 그래서 안 낫
고 덧났던 거야. 새로 사온 이 연고 발라 보고도 안 듣거
든 그때는 불치병이라고 우겨도 좋다. 알았지? 여보세요!
여보세요! 섭아! 영섭아!"

살뜰히 타이르고 있던 숙희가 벌컥 소리를 지르고는 송
수화기를 내려놓았다.

"그놈의 자식은 또 무슨 헛소리야?"

"오늘밤에도 친구 자취방에서 자겠답니다. 절대로 방송

der over it like snow. To affect future enemies rather than current ones, they spray defoliants. They can't defoliate and burn down forests to push humans and animals out on the same day. Also, they ruthlessly spray CS powder and defoliants in areas where infantrymen can't carry out operations.

Ik-su knew what was going on under the helicopter while he was sitting in it. He could confirm how effective the powder and defoliants were through radio communications. People were frantically running out, collapsing, covering their mouths with their clothes, staggering and reeling like drunkards; there were two women holding babies and three women with children who were welcoming Agent Orange with outstretched arms as if it were snow. Reports came in fast and thick like the broadcast of an amusing play.

Trained with CS powder, Ik-su made light of Agent Orange. To him, if the asphyxiant gas was like agrichemicals, defoliants were like fertilizers. In fact, he sprayed defoliants like fertilizers when they were eradicating forests near their base. Dense forests near the base frightened officers and their men. The enemy could sneak in and stage an ambush there. They couldn't deal with those forests

에는 안 나갈 거니까 모레 저녁쯤에나 생각해보고 집에 가겠다, 이러고는 전화를 끊네요."

"그 자식 누가 방송에 얼굴 비치라고 시켰나. 그 시간에는 학교에 있을 놈이."

"이름을 대거나 사진이 나오게 하면 집에는 절대 안 들어오겠다고, 가출 선언을 하네요."

"뭐라고? 새 연고 바르고 낫기만 나아라. 그놈의 자식, 가출이 아니라 출가를 시키지."

숙희는 그저께 통조림 공장에서 퇴근하는 길에 읍내 약국을 찾았다. 뚱뚱한 의사가 적어준 영어 쪽지를 약사에게 보여줬다. 어머니는 의사의 장담과 새 연고를 불치의 병에서 작은놈을 구원해줄 구세주처럼 믿고 있었다.

"정말 안 드실 겁니까? 정말 안 먹을 거야?"

숙희가 남편과 아들을 번갈아 쏘아보았다.

"일찌감치 누울래."

"엄마, 나도."

숙희가 내던질 기세로 밥상을 들어올렸다.

using scythes as in Korea. It was hardly an exaggeration to say that the forests in Vietnam grew right back after the soldiers who had just cut them down turned away. Naturally, defoliants made in the USA and brought by the chemical soldier were very popular. Ik-su played the role of instructor in the forest removal operation near the base, commanding a platoon, including guards. He modeled the way to spray the defoliant by holding a steel helmet full of it next to his chest with his left hand and spraying a fistful of it over the rapidly growing plants with his right. The silly soldiers clapped. They were probably thankful for this problem-solver who was saving them from the sweaty labor of weeding.

*

Suk-hui cooked some abalone porridge for dinner. She didn't seel two palm-sized abalones, just for her son. Husband and wife were sitting on the floor at the low table, and Yeong-ho was sitting in his wheelchair using Yeong-seop's chair as his table. Ik-su complimented Suk-hui on the soup's delicious taste, and Suk-hui said that it was salted just right. But Yeong-ho kept staring at his bowl on top of his

*

　고단한 사람들이 내일의 벅찬 일거리에 대비해 충분한 휴식을 누리려는 것일까? 익수네는 일찍 불이 꺼졌다. 문 지방에서부터 익수, 숙희, 영호의 차례로 누운 그들은 끈덕지게 입을 다물고 있었다. 벙어리 가족 같았다.

　숙희는 평소보다 거칠게 쌕쌕거리는 남편의 숨소리가 불안했다. 자꾸만 불길한 예감에 시달리고 있었다. 그것이 일 년 만에 또다시 찾아오려는가. 죽음의 예행 연습, 참혹한 의식(儀式)의 전조일지 모른다는 생각이 스쳐갈 때는 심장이 멈추는 듯했다.

　숙희는 방을 벗어나고 싶었다. 원망할 상대, 하소연할 상대를 만나고 싶었다. 그러나 떠오르는 얼굴이 없었다. 문득 뻐꾸기가 생각났다. 그놈의 뻐꾸기, 그놈의 뻐꾸기를 잡아서 모가지를 비틀든가 해야지. 숙희는 그놈의 모가지만 비틀어 버린다면 남편이 몸서리치는 연중행사를 모면할 수 있을 것 같았다. 그러나 잠시였다. 뻐꾸기를 없애겠다는 터무니없는 집착이 스러지자 지끈지끈하고 어질어질했다. 징그러운 벌레가 머릿속에서 제멋대로 설치는 증상이었다.

brother's chair as if observing it. After stealing a few glances at what he was doing, his parents couldn't help commenting.

"What are you up to?"

"Hurry up! It must be about the right temperature for eating now."

Yeong-ho sighed over the abalone porridge, "This rare delicacy doesn't become flesh for father and it only becomes shit for me!"

"Hey, why are you doing this today? You upset me before with Zhuangzi and skeletons... Did you think I couldn't understand because I'm ignorant? You really want to be this way?"

"Well, please fully enjoy the soup, Father!"

"Why are you making me so angry? I can't eat any more!" Shouting abruptly, Ik-su put down his spoon.

"Why are you doing this, too?" protested Suk-hui. But she was glaring at her son. Yeong-ho wore the same smile he had during the day, a smile that seemed to boast of his sage-like transcendence of the ordinary.

"Fine, if you're going to starve, let's all starve together." After slamming down her spoon, Suk-hui stood up fiercely and moved Yeong-ho's bowl to

125

밥벌레, 죽음도 비켜가는 밥벌레. 숙희는 남편의 품에 안겨 사죄의 눈물을 흘렸으나 스스로 용서되지 않았다. 이른바 국민이 지켜보는 앞에서 아내가 병든 남편을 밥벌레라 지칭한 사실이 참담했다. 아침부터 저녁까지 몸살이 덤빌 틈도 용납하지 않으며 암초를 뒤지고 통조림 공장으로 뛰어갔던 그 세월의 당당한 긍지와 자부심을, 카메라 앞에서 자기 손으로 유리병처럼 내동댕이친 것이었다.

숙희가 모로 누웠다. 아들이 가슴 앞에 있었다. 영호는 엎드린 채 숨소리만 내고 있었다. 모름지기 따뜻한 말이 그리웠다. 아들의 등에 손을 얹었다.

"영호야, 자나?"

"자야지."

"기도원에서는 몇 시에 자나?"

"정한 시간 없다. 자고 싶으면 자고, 멀뚱거리고 싶으면 멀뚱거리고, 그러는 거지 뭐."

아들이 심드렁해서 어머니는 더 살뜰히 굴었다.

"왜 밥은 잘 안 먹나? 배고프지? 지금이라도 차려줄까?"

"건너뛰고 싶다. 맨날 하는 큰일이 밥 먹고 잠자고 똥오줌 내는 일이고, 그 중에서 제일 큰 행사가 똥을 내는 일

126

the table.

"Forget about broadcasting or whatever! Go back to the prayer house tomorrow morning! You shouldn't come home if you aren't going to talk, just smile and starve. You came to upset your parents? I don't want to see you. Don't you feel sympathy for your mother?" Ik-su ruthlessly poured out cruel words toward his son. He was choked up with emotion. He couldn't breathe.

"Are you OK? You'll have a hard time again like this. Please calm down. Please!"

"I don't have the strength to speak any more. Take away the table! I want to lie down."

Having a hard time breathing, Ik-su was panting.

"Ho, why are you doing this? Did you really come to upset us?"

"I wanted to listen to the cuckoos crying." Looking at his mother, Yeong-ho smiled.

"Does that make any sense? There's a nice forest at the Gospel Prayer House, too. Are there no cuckoos there?"

"Mom, let's stop. Help me lie down. I'd like to sleep."

Suk-hui was about to slap him across the face, when the phone rang loudly.

인데, 밥을 한 번 쉬면 똥도 한 번 쉬게 되겠지."

"호야, 엄마 속이 찢어지는 걸 보자고 자꾸 그런 소리나 하나?"

"뭐, 그냥."

"아버지 때문에 섭섭해서 그러나? 그게 아버지 진심이 겠나? 아들이 밥도 안 먹고 삐딱한 소리나 해대니까 서운 하신 거지. 안 그래도 너한테 죄 지은 사람처럼 속으로는 항상 쩔쩔매는 양반인데."

"죄는 무슨 죄. 시대를 잘못 만났던 거지."

"제발 기운 좀 내라. 우리 서로 포기하는 마음은 먹지 말자. 의사가 그랬잖아. 인체는 신비하다고. 어느 순간에 거짓말같이 그렇게 된 것처럼 어느 순간에 거짓말같이 회 생될 수 있다고. 기도도 열심히 하고, 그런 순간이 꼭 온 다는 믿음부터 가지자."

"돌팔이의 무책임한 소리지."

"내가 보기에는 니가 니한테 무책임해 보인다. 왜 밥도 안 먹고 버티나?"

숙희가 살짝 나무랐다.

"내가 무슨 사육되는 짐승인가? 밥 적게 먹고 저녁 한 끼 굶은 것 가지고 왜 이리 야단이고? 나도 사람이다. 밥

"Seop? Where are you?"

Ik-su and Yeong-ho darted a glances at the receiver.

"All right, I know you haven't missed school. I checked. Seop, I don't need your excuses. Just come home. Your brother is here, too. Don't you want to see your brother? Your father is so angry that he wants to send him back tomorrow morning. I bought a new medicine for you. Hurry up! It will be a while until the last bus, you know."

Yeong-seop went to school on a 7:10 A.M. village shuttle bus and got off around 7 P.M. every day. An exemplary student who had never been late for school even in rain or snow, he was calling home for the first time in days to let his parents know that he was going to stay away from home for a fifth night. The wrinkles around his mother's eyes deepened, as she listened to her youngest son.

"Trust that doctor. You'd only applied ointment for eczema and hadn't seen a dermatologist. Why is it incurable? He said it's not eczema, but ringworm, didn't he? Didn't he say the ointment for eczema made ringworm worse? He's right, isn't he? That was why it was getting worse, not better. If you don't get better after applying this new ointment, it's OK

먹기 싫을 때도 있는 것이 정상이잖아?"

영호가 노골적으로 짜증을 부렸다. 숙희가 홱 몸을 돌렸다. 젊은 시절에 기분 상한 잠자리에서 남편의 손길을 거부하던 때처럼 꼭 그렇게. 못된 놈. 콧잔등이 시큰했으나 입술을 다물었다. 그 찰나였다. 숙희의 내면에 어떤 옹벽이 무너지고 있었다. 짧은 동안의 연쇄 폭발처럼 격렬한 진동이 일어났다. 그러나 숙희는 덤덤했다. 대뜸 그 사단을 알아차렸다. 십여 년에 걸쳐 공들여 쌓은 탑이 눈 깜짝하는 사이에 와르르 무너진 것이었다. 방 안에는 아무런 탈이 없었다. 익수의 거친 숨소리만 아니라면 어둔 침묵에 싸여 있었다.

숙희는 헤아렸다. 사실은 오래 전에 그 탑이 무너졌는데 다만 인정하기 싫었던 거라고 해야 옳았다. 숙희는 인정했다. 지난 며칠 동안 밤마다 자신을 물어뜯은 밥벌레가 텔레비전 카메라 앞에서 난데없이 튀어나온 것이 아니었다. 전쟁의 후유증에 시달려서 서서히 죽어가는 남편을 산야의 병든 짐승처럼 방치해온 나라를 향해 자신의 원통한 심정을 더 간절히 나타내려다 보니 그 몹쓸 말을 입에 담았다고 변명할 수 있겠지만, 그러나 수사적 기교를 의식하지 못한 상태에서 그 말이 튀어나왔고, 그것이야말로

for you to insist that it's incurable. Got it? Hello! Hello! Seop! Yeong-seop!" Suk-hui put down the receiver, after abruptly yelling right in the middle of this attempt at affectionate persuasion.

"What nonsense is that bastard saying?"

"He said he was going to stay with his friend. Since he would never agree to be interviewed, he said he'd only come back in two days—and he was thinking that over, too. Then he hung up."

"Who told him to give an interview? Besides, he'll be at school during that time the day after tomorrow."

"If we even mention his name or give them his photo, then he'll never come back. That's what he declared."

"What? Let's see what he says, if he gets better with that new ointment. Even if he doesn't run away from home, why don't we marry him off and kick him out!"

Suk-hui went to the downtown pharmacy on her way home from the canning factory. She showed the note written in English by the doctor to the pharmacist. The mother in her saw the doctor as a savior and believed his assertion that the new ointment would rescue her youngest son from an incur-

아내로서 어머니로서 지칠 대로 지쳐 있었다는 명백한 증
거였다.

*

동그란 탁상시계가 막 자정을 넘었다. 영섭과 두 친구
는 소주의 마지막 잔을 남겨두었다. 네모난 밥상 위의 냄
비에는 불어터진 오뎅 몇 토막이 남았다. 영섭의 눈두덩
은 그 오뎅처럼 부풀었다. 그러나 셋은 여전히 눈빛이 반
들반들 빛나고 있었다. 볼이 붉게 물들었지만 두어 시간
전에 자취방으로 들어올 때와 마찬가지로 심각하고 진지
한 표정이었다.

"영섭아, 진짜 친구로서 마지막 부탁이다. 니가 어른처
럼 행동해라. 아버님이 유명해지자고 그러셨겠나. 비슷한
처지에 놓인 전우들을 돕고 싶고, 또 당신의 억울함도 세
상에 하소연을 하셨던 거지."

방의 주인이 야무지게 말했다.

"내가 그 점을 의심했나?"

그가 얼른 받아쳤다.

"그러면 됐다. 계집애 그거? 재수 없다, 하고는 잊어버

132

able disease.

"So you really won't eat? You, too?"

Suk-hui scowled at her husband and then her son.

"I'll have to go to bed now."

"Mom, me, too."

Suk-hui picked up the table as if she was about to throw it away.

*

Maybe these exhausted people were just trying to get enough rest to face the next day's overwhelming tasks. The lights went out early at Ik-su's house. Ik-su, Suk-hui, and Yeong-ho, lying in that order from the door, remained obstinately silent. They resembled a family of mutes.

Suk-hui was worried about her husband panting more than usual. She continued to have bad premonitions. *Is it going to visit us again this year?* Wondering if this was a sign for the rehearsal of death, that cruel ritual, her heart sank.

Suk-hui wanted to leave the room. She wished there was someone she could complain or to appeal to. But she couldn't picture anybody. Suddenly she remembered the cuckoos. *Damn cuckoos! Maybe I*

려라. 그런 계집애는 어차피 날라리과다. 니 어머님과는 정반대다. 차라리 잘됐다고 생각해라."

영섭이 소주잔을 집었다. 저녁에 만나 통닭을 사이좋게 뜯어먹고 해수욕장으로 나가 팔짱을 끼고 거닐었던 갸름한 얼굴이 메추리알만 하게 축소돼서 소주잔 속으로 풍당 빠지는가 싶더니 별안간 소주잔이 요강만 하게 팽창하다 가뭇없이 사라졌다. 홀연히 영섭은 갸름한 얼굴을 오른손에 쥐고 있었다. 그 사랑의 요술을 감당하기 벅찼다. 사납게 소주를 삼켰다.

1학년 겨울방학 때 미팅에서 만나 여섯 달째 사귀어온 여상(女商) 2학년 강미영. 계집애는 자신감이 넘쳐나고, 머슴애는 주눅 들듯이 얌전하다. 그 성격 차이가 오히려 상대의 허한 구석을 채워주는지 둘은 날이 갈수록 가까워졌다. 요새는 작별키스 따위에 스스럼이 없었다.

166에 46. 이것은 미영이 자랑하는 수치다. 키와 몸무게가 말해주듯 가냘프다는 인상을 풍기는 날씬한 몸매와 예쁘장한 계란형 얼굴, 이 육체적 조건이 미영에게는 미래에 대한 자신감을 제공하는 원천이었다. 바라는 미래는 단순했다. 여상을 졸업하면 취직할 수 있고, 언제든 자신이 마음만 먹으면 괜찮은 남자를 남편으로 찍을 수 있다

should catch those damn cuckoos and wring their necks... Suk-hui felt as if she could prevent her husband's terrifying annual ritual by wringing the necks of all the cuckoos. But that thought just flitted by. As soon as her nonsensical obsession with killing off cuckoos had passed, her head throbbed and she felt dizzy. It felt as if some creepy worm was randomly crawling everywhere inside her brain.

A useless mouth, a useless mouth that even death fears and avoids... Suk-hui couldn't forgive herself for saying that, even after shedding tears of apology in her husband's arms. She felt miserable for becoming a wife who called her sick husband a useless mouth in front of the whole country. She had tossed away her own pride and dignity that made her run around all day, rummaging through the reefs and running to the canning company, never giving in to fatigue—she threw it all away herself, in front of the camera, like some empty bottles.

Suk-hui lay sideways. Her son was in front. Lying face down, Yeong-ho was only making breathing sounds. She missed the sound of caring words. She put her hand on his back.

"Yeong-ho, are you sleeping?"

는 것이다.

영섭도 공고생이니까 취업은 문제가 아니었다. 신체적 조건도 빠지는 데가 없다. 178에 66이다. 얼굴은 청년 시절의 아버지처럼 미남형이다. 조금 어둠침침한 성품이 흠이라면 흠이다. 그러나 미영은 그 점을 싸안아주면서 존재감을 더 빛내는 형이다.

"섭아, 잊어버려라."

영섭의 짝꿍이 거들었다. 방의 주인이 더 세게 나왔다.

"그 계집애, 사실은 깡통이잖아. 니가 한 번 눌러버렸더라면 시들시들해졌을 거다."

영섭은 두 친구의 충고를 먼 메아리처럼 희미하게 들었다. 미영의 또랑또랑한 목소리가 귓전에 맴돌고 있었다. 어젯밤에 한숨도 못 자고 생각해 봤는데, 너의 그 습진 말이야. 그것도 이젠 예삿일 같지가 않아. 영섭이가 아버님처럼 형님처럼 변할 수도 있다고 상상하니까 끔찍스러워 죽겠어. 우연히 그 뉴스를 보고는 얼마나 놀랐는지 알아? 늦게라도 형님 얘기까지 솔직하게 말해줘서 고마워. 넌 정말 좋은 애야. 하지만 난 불안해. 불안해 하면서 계속 사귀기는 싫어. 날 이해해줘. 영섭은 해변 도로에서 택시를 잡아타는 미영의 뒷모습만 멍하니 바라보았다. 이름도

"I'd better."

"What time do you usually go to bed in the prayer house?"

"There's no set time. If you want to sleep, you can sleep. If you want to stare blankly into space, you can do that, too."

Because her son seemed so uninterested, she became even more caring.

"Why didn't you eat? You're hungry, aren't you? Why don't I set the table?"

"I want to skip it. My biggest task every day is to eat, to sleep, and to pee and shit. The biggest task is shitting. So if I skip a meal, then I guess I'll skip shitting once."

"Ho, are you saying that to completely break your mom's heart?"

"No, it has no meaning."

"Are you upset because of your father? Do you think that's what your father really means? He was upset because you, his son, weren't eating and being sarcastic. Deep down he feels so terribly sorry, as if this was all his fault."

"What fault? We were just born at the wrong time."

"Please cheer up. Let's not give up. Didn't the doctor say that the human body is a very mysterious

부르지 못했다.

"섭아, 인제 정신 차려라. 마음부터 다잡아라."

"섭아, 그 의사 말 믿고 어머님이 사다놨다는 약부터 발라 봐라. 그래서 그 불안과 공포부터 벗어던져라. 안 그러면 임마, 너는 평생 동안 마음 병신으로 살게 될 거다."

"맞다. 그 깡통을 아까워할 때가 아니다. 사타구니에 바르는 약부터 바꿔라. 자, 자, 조금씩 나눠서 막잔을 기분 좋게 쨍 하자."

두 친구가 영섭의 빈 잔에다 자기 잔의 소주를 몇 방울씩 따랐다.

"내일은 집에 들어가라. 알았지?"

방의 주인이 다짐을 받고, 짝꿍이 소주잔을 높였다.

"새꺄, 막잔 제끼자. 깡통도 차버리고 마음 병도 차버리기, 위하여!"

영섭은 무겁게 소주잔을 올렸다.

*

"아악!"

숙희가 비명을 질렀다. 입에서 피를 질질 흘리는 익수

138

thing? That you might recover all of a sudden just the way you became ill all of a sudden? Let's pray hard. Let's first believe that a moment like that must come."

"That's just a quack being irresponsible."

"To me you look irresponsible to yourself. Why are you refusing to eat?" Suk-hui scolded him gently.

"Am I some sort of domestic animal? Why are you making such a fuss about my eating less and skipping just one dinner? I'm a human being, too. Isn't it normal for me to feel like not eating once in a while?"

Yeong-ho acted openly annoyed. Suk-hui abruptly turned away—just as she had in bed in the old days when she was upset with her husband and rejected his advances. *Bastard!* She was moved to tears, but kept her mouth tightly shut. At that moment an impregnable wall finally started collapsing inside her. A shock wave, as violent as one from quick, successive explosions, went through her body. But Suk-hui remained calm. She realized right away what had just happened. The pagoda she had been building with great effort for the past ten years had come tumbling down in an instant. The room

가 형형한 눈을 부릅뜨고 덤벼드는 찰나, 요행히 눈을 떴다. 악몽을 벗어난 몸은 땀에 젖었다. 그러나 숙희는 옆구리가 허전한 느낌부터 받았다. 손을 뻗다가 소스라쳤다.

"왝! 왝!"

방문 앞, 쪽마루였다. 화들짝 일어난 숙희가 외등 스위치를 올렸다. 피비린내가 코를 찔렀다. 익수는 사기요강에 얼굴을 박고 있었다.

"여보!"

숙희가 등을 토닥였다. 익수는 일부러 그러듯 모로 쓰러졌다. 요강에는 검붉은 피가 홍건했다. 한 그릇은 될 것 같았다. 숙희는 놀라지 않았다. 침착하게 남편을 반듯이 눕혔다. 해골 같은 얼굴에 빛이 쏟아졌다. 입가에 피가 묻어 있었다. 숙희는 손바닥으로 닦았다. 익수가 눈꺼풀을 힘겹게 움직였다.

"추워요? 방으로 들어갈래요?"

"괜찮다. 꿈을, 꿨다."

"꿈을요? 나도요. 잘 아는 사람이 무섭게 나왔어요. 당신은요?"

익수가 앙상한 팔을 저었다. 괴롭다, 묻지 마라. 숙희는 뜻을 읽었다. 그는 짧았던 토막 꿈을 환각처럼 다시 보고

looked fine. It was wrapped in silence except for Ik-su's panting.

Suk-hui thought for a moment. It would have been more accurate to say she had been refusing to accept that the pagoda had already collapsed a long time ago. She was just acknowledging it now. The phrase "useless mouth" that had nagged at her conscience didn't just accidentally fly out of her mouth. She might make the excuse that she only used that phrase to express her resentment toward the government that had been neglecting her husband's slow and painful death from the aftereffects of the war. But when the phrase came out of her mouth she wasn't thinking about some rhetorical strategy, so it was clear that she was at her tattered wit's end as wife and mother.

*

The hands of the round clock on the table pointed just past midnight. Yeong-seop and his two friends had only one glass of *soju* each left in front of them. There were a few puffy fish sausages in the pot on the low, square table. Yeong-seop's eyes were as puffy as the fish sausage. But the eyes of all three

있었다. 십여 미터 앞에서 시뻘건 불길이 달려온다. 수평의 폭포 같다. 그가 겁에 질려 뒷걸음을 치지만 몸이 고정돼 있다. 불길이 뱉은 것처럼 두 사내가 튀어나온다. 두 사내는 낮은 공중에서 마구 헛바퀴를 굴린다. 박문현 대위와 죽은 전우다. 사자의 이름이 생각나지 않는다. 산 자와 죽은 자가 서로 먼저 도망치려고 필사적으로 허둥대는 꼴이다. 아니다. 영호와 영섭이다. 형제가 아버지에게 살려 달라고 아우성을 친다. 아니다. 두 아들은 아니다. 낯설다. 아, 베트남 청년이다. 구덩이에 숨어 있다가 익수의 화염방사기를 맞고 혼비백산 뛰쳐나온 두 청년이다. 불길을 도망치는 것이 아니다. 익수를 잡으려고 불길을 이끌고 달려오는 형세다. 아아아……. 익수가 사지를 오그리며 비명을 지른다. 그러나 혀가 안으로 말려들며 숨이 멈춘다. 퍼뜩 그가 눈을 떴다. 이미 핏덩이가 목구멍에 고여 있었다.

"마아, 그때, 연장 근무, 할거로야."

익수가 해묵은 후회를 뱉었다. 느닷없이 까무러쳤다가 의식이 돌아온 다음에는 회복의 한 절차처럼 솟아나던 것이었다. 방금도 그는 얼핏 베트남의 마지막을 생각했다. 박문현 대위는 익수가 귀국할 때가 다가오니까 베트남 근

boys were still bright. Although their faces were flushed, their expressions were still as serious as when they entered the room.

"Yeong-seop, as your dear friend, I am asking you for the last time to act like an adult. Do you think your father went on TV to become famous? He wanted to help other veterans in a similar situation, and to show the world his frustrations," said the owner of the room firmly.

"Do you think I doubt that?" Yeong-seop retorted.

"That's all that matters. That chick? Remember she's bad luck, and forget her! A chick like that, interested only in fun, is no use in the end. She's the opposite of your mother. Consider it a blessing."

Yeong-seop picked up his *soju* glass. The oval face of that girl, with whom he lovingly shared a roast chicken in the evening and walked arm-in-arm on the beach, became as small as a quail and dropped with a plop into his glass. Then it started expanding to the size of a chamber pot, and vanished. All of a sudden, Yeong-seop was holding that slender oval face in his right hand. He was having a hard time, overwhelmed by the magic of love. He forcefully gulped down more *soju*.

He met Kang Mi-yeong, a junior at a girls' com-

무를 연장할 수 없겠느냐고 했다. 명령은 아니었다. 권유였다. 너 같은 베테랑을 어디 가서 구하겠느냐고 꼬드기기도 했다. 익수는 마음이 기울곤 했다. 그러나 거절하고 말았다. 월맹군의 구정 공세에 아군이 한방 오지게 얻어맞은 때여서 겁이 났고, 고향에서 끈덕지게 편지를 보내오는 숙희가 그리웠다. 박 대위는 진심으로 아쉬워했다. 그의 손목에는 제일 비싼 걸로 골랐다는 세이코 시계를 걸어주고, 그의 마음에는 오래 남은 말을 걸어주었다. 사람이 어떤 선택을 하고 나면 운명이 정해준 장소에서 인내하고 투쟁해야 한다. 익수는 박 대위의 권유를 피한 것이 자기 운명의 장소를 피한 것만 같았다. 월남에 더 눌러 있다가 어느 밀림에서 죽어야 하는 운명이었던 것을……. 이 후회가 빈사 상태에서도 송곳처럼 의식을 후비고 있다.

"마음부터 흔들리진 말아요. 왜 안 깨웠어요?"

숙희가 남편을 나무랐다.

"인제는, 정말로, 조용히, 죽어버리면, 좋겠구나."

익수가 띄엄띄엄 말을 마쳤다.

"당신이 죽기는 왜 죽어요? 병명도 모르고 병인도 모르는데 억울해서라도 어떻게 죽어요?"

mercial, on a group blind date in the winter of his freshman year in high school. She was full of self-confidence and he was as quiet as someone who had already lost his heart. Perhaps because they complemented each other, they became closer with each meeting. Then they began exchanging farewell kisses.

166cm and 46kg—these numbers were the source of Mi-yeong's pride, for they described her body. That body and her pretty face were the source of her confidence in her future. Her aspirations were simple. She would get a job after graduating from high school and then marry with any decent guy she liked, whenever she wanted.

Since Yeong-seop was going to a technical high school, he had no problem getting a job. He was a good-looking guy, too. He was 178cm tall and weighed 66kg. He had a handsome face like his father's when he was young. The only drawback was his rather somber disposition. Mi-yeong was the right type of person for him, someone who could accept his drawback and make him shine.

"Seop, forget her," added Yeong-seop's buddy. The room's owner was harsher: "Frankly, that chick was an airhead. If you pushed it hard, it would

영호는 기척이 없었다. 마치 혼절해서 엎어진 사람 같
았다.

"병원, 안 간다, 절대⋯⋯."

숙희는 남편의 의식이 닫히는 것을 직감했다. 병원이
급했다. 영호의 머리맡을 비켜서 전화통으로 다가갔다.
벽시계가 새벽 2시에 다가서고 있었다. 읍내 택시를 불러
야 한다. 숙희는 너무 먼 앰뷸런스를 포기했다. 그만큼 정
신이 가지런했다. 전화통 밑에서 전화번호 쪽지를 집어내
외등 불빛 쪽으로 몸을 돌렸다.

신호가 가고 있다. 한 번, 두 번, 세 번⋯⋯. 숙희는 초
조해진다. 혹시 모두가 자리를 비운 게 아닌가. 다행히 일
곱 번 만에 굵은 목소리가 나왔다.

"호미곶 김익수 씨 집입니다."

"아, 예. 고엽제 환자."

"급합니다. 빨리 오세요. 응급실로 가야 합니다."

"또 넘어갔어요? 준비하세요. 총알같이 갑니다!"

"바로 집 앞에 공터까지 올라와주세요. 차에 태워줄 사
람이 없어요."

"예. 알았어요."

숙희는 송수화기를 내려놓고 숨을 돌렸다. 익수는 죽은

have wilted right away."

To Yeong-seop's ears, his friends' advice was a vague echo from far away. Mi-yeong's clear voice was still ringing in his ears. *I was thinking all last night. You know, your eczema, I think it might not be normal eczema. I'm terrified. What if you become like your father or brother? I happened to see the news. Do you know how surprised I was? Thank you for telling me honestly about your brother. You're a good person. But I'm afraid. I don't want to see you, feeling scared like this. Please understand.* Yeong-seop stared blankly at Mi-yeong's back as she was getting into a taxi on the seaside road. He couldn't even call out her name.

"Seop, wake up! You have to be strong!"

"Seop, trust the doctor and try that ointment your mother got. Get rid of those anxieties and fears first! If you don't, you'll live as a mentally disabled person your whole life."

"That's right. There's no time to miss that airhead. Change the ointment for your groin first. Hey, here, take this *soju* and let's toast our last glass!"

Each friend poured a few drop of *soju* from his glass into Yeong-seop's empty one.

"Go home tomorrow, OK?"

듯이 드러누워 있고, 영호는 죽은 듯이 엎드려 있다. 숙희는 이를 악물었다. 남편을 외면했다. 아들도 외면했다. 그래야 떠날 준비를 할 수 있을 듯했다.

숙희는 텔레비전 받침대에 딸린 서랍을 열었다. 영세민 의료보험카드를 챙기고, 통조림 공장에서 받은 품삯을 손지갑에 넣었다. 우선 그 돈이면 응급실에서 쫓겨나지는 않을 것이었다. 벽에 걸린 옷을 벗겼다. 장바닥에서 골라 잡은 헐렁한 청바지와 연두색 긴소매 남방. 통조림 공장 출근길의 흔한 옷차림이다. 빨래를 해둔 것이어서 비린내는 없었다. 옷을 갈아입고 빠뜨린 게 없는가를 헤아렸다. 요강이 눈에 띄었다. 저걸 비우고 씻어둬야지. 이 생각에 따르려다 동작을 뚝 멈췄다. 호리호리한 기자가 다시 찾아오겠다고 했으니 저걸 놔두자. 내일인데 그냥 덮어놓자. 더 처참한 모습을 원한다면 바로 이때 올 것이지. 숙희는 괜히 분통이 터졌다.

"흐음, 흐음."

문득 영호가 마른기침을 했다. 숙희는 다음을 기다렸다. 생리 현상의 처리를 부탁할 것이라고 생각했다. 하지만 아들은 말이 없었다. 아버지를 걱정하는 말도, 다른 어떤 말도 하지 않았다. 단지 심심해서 살아 있다는 신호를

The room's owner urged Yeong-seop to promise and his buddy raised his glass high.

"Dude, Let's drink it all up. This is our last glass. To dumping that peabrain and to chasing off mental problems, cheers!"

Yeong-seop sluggishly raised his glass.

*

"AAAAAH!" Suk-hui screamed. She was lucky enough to open her eyes the moment Ik-su was jumping at her and glaring fiercely, blood flowing from his mouth. Waking from this nightmare, Suk-hui was completely soaked in sweat. But even before that, Suk-hui had sensed an absence beside her. While groping around with her hand, she was suddenly surprised by a loud noise.

"Gyaarrrgh!"

The sound was coming from the narrow veranda in front of the room. Jumping up, Suk-hui turned on the outdoor light. She was overcome by the smell of blood. Ik-su was burying his face in the porcelain chamber pot.

"Honey!"

Suk-hui patted his back. Ik-su was collapsed on

보낸 것 같았다. 묵묵히 녹음기만 지켜보고 있었다. 그러나 숙희는 아들에게 힘을 빼지 않기로 했다.

"호야, 저 요강은 안 비우고 변소에 가져가서 잘 덮어놓는다. 혹시 내가 없는 사이에 기자가 오고 의사가 오면 아버지가 토한 피라고 알려줘라. 찍어가든지 가져가서 검사를 하든지, 삶아 먹든지 데쳐 먹든지, 좋은 대로 하라고 해라. 아버지는 늘 가던 병원에 간다. 들었냐?"

영호가 턱을 위아래로 움직였다. 요강을 치운 숙희가 다시 방으로 들어왔다. 빼먹은 하나가 생각난 것이었다. 전화통을 영호의 손이 쉽게 닿는 지점으로 옮겼다. 전화 받는 아들이 낑낑대지 않게 해주려는 배려였다.

"호야, 아침까지 전화 없거든 아버지가 이번에도 무사한 줄 알아라. 그럴 리야 만무하지만, 만약 아버지한테 특별한 변고가 생기면 그때는 바로 전화할게."

숙희는 일부러 진지하게 일렀다. 제발 아버지에게 관심을 좀 가지라는 뜻이었다. 영호가 고개를 오른쪽으로 조금 비틀어서 전화통을 뚫어지게 쏘아보았다. 그러나 입가에는 빙긋이 웃음을 지었다.

"우리 아버지, 안 죽는 사람이잖아. 곧 돌아가실 것같이 저러고 계시다가 잠을 깨는 것처럼 일어나신 게 한두 번

his side as if on purpose. The chamber pot was full of blackish-red blood. It seemed as if it would fill an entire bowl. Suk-hui wasn't surprised. She calmly laid him down on his back. Light was pouring onto his skeletal face. There was blood around his mouth. Suk-hui wiped it off with her palm. Ik-su slowly opened his eyelids.

"Are you cold? Do you want to go back to the room?"

"That's OK. I had a dream."

"A dream? I had one, too. Someone I know very well appeared and he looked scary. How about you?"

Ik-su waved his scrawny arm. *I'm in pain. Don't ask me.* Suk-hui could understand. He was looking at snapshots of his dream like illusions. *A red-hot flame is running toward him. It looks like a vertical waterfall. Scared, he's trying to walk backward but his body won't move. Two guys jump out of the flames as if vomited. They spin wildly in mid-air. It's Capt. Bak Mun-hyeon and a dead fellow soldier. He can't remember the dead guy's name. The living and the dead are desperately trying to run away. No, it's Yeong-ho and Yeong-seop. The brothers are pleading desperately for their father to rescue them. No, they*

151

이었나. 이번에도 몇 시간 뒤에는 또 멀쩡하게 살아나시 겠지 뭐."

숙희는 울화통이 치밀었다. 너무 무덤덤한 아들의 엉덩이를 갈겨주지 못하는 격정이 얼굴을 불덩이로 만들었다. 아들도 남편도 보기 싫었다. 택시를 마중하러 나가듯이 대문을 벗어났다. 그제야 숙희는 얼굴을 두 손바닥에 묻었다. 울지 않으려고 안간힘을 짜냈다. 길바닥에 주저앉았다. 익수가 영호의 승합차를 기다리던 그 자리였다. 어려울 때는 즐거웠던 때를 회상하라. 숙희는 하루에도 몇 번씩 되뇌는 생활의 훈(訓)을 불러왔다. 그것은 혼자만 알고 꽁꽁 숨겨둔 행복의 금고를 따는 열쇠와 같았다. 회상이나 추억, 그 공간을 흐르는 시간은 얼마나 빠른가. 연애 시절, 신혼 시절을 잠깐 쉬는 동안에도 두루 돌아다닐 수 있었다.

*

이웃 동네의 처녀와 총각으로 만난 숙희와 익수는 그의 입대 전부터 눈이 맞은 사이였다. 숙희는 그가 맹호부대에 자원하는 것을 반대했다. 천금보다도 당신을 원한다는

are not his two sons. They look foreign. Ah, they are the two young Vietnamese men. They aren't running away from the flames. They're running after Ik-su to catch him, ahead of the flames. Ahhh... Curling up, Ik-su screams. But his tongue is rolling back, and he can't breathe.

Suddenly, he opened his eyes. His throat was already full of blood.

"I should have extended my stay in Vietnam..." Ik-su spat out his belated regret. This thought always sprang up like a step toward recovery whenever he revived after suddenly losing consciousness. He was just thinking of the last days of his tour of duty. When Ik-su was about to be discharged, Capt. Bak asked him if he wouldn't like to extend his stay in Vietnam. It wasn't an order, just a request. He also tried to seduce him, asking where else he could find a veteran like Ik-su. Ik-su felt somewhat tempted. But in the end he refused. He was scared because the Korean army had just received a huge blow from the Lunar New Year offensive by the North Vietnamese Army. He also missed Suk-hui, who had continued to write him letters. Capt. Bak really regretted his leaving. He put the most expensive Seiko watch that he specially got for Ik-su on

소망이었다. 그러나 익수는 듣지 않았다. 월남에 가서 한 밑천 잡고 고향으로 돌아와서, 기름쟁이 생활은 청산하고 목공소 차려서 새 출발을 하겠다는 것이었다.

숙희는 전쟁터의 익수에게 한 달에 세 번은 꼬박꼬박 편지를 띄우고, 익수는 세 번에 두 번은 답신을 띄웠다. 사랑해요. 사랑해. 이 말을 둘은 편지에 뺀 적이 없었다. 정작 가정을 꾸린 뒤에는 서로 쑥스러워서 꺼내지도 못했 지만, 편지의 달콤한 고백이 둘의 사랑을 가꾸고 키워준 은인이었다.

익수가 부산항에 돌아온 날, 숙희는 마중을 나갔다. 재 회하는 그의 모습이 딴사람 같았다. 얼굴이 딸기처럼 빨 갛게 익어 있었고 몸이 홀쭉해 보였다. 하지만 무조건 반 갑고 무조건 감격스러웠다. 그런 변화에 민감할 틈이 없 었다. 워낙 더운 나라에서 햇볕을 많이 쬐고 땀을 많이 흘 려서 그러려니 하고 말았다.

1968년 3월 귀국해서 4월에 제대한 익수의 몸무게는 겨 우 54kg이었다. 그리고 달포가 지났다. 호미곶 보리밭이 누렇게 물들고 있는 달밤이었다. 무덤가에서 숙희를 품은 그가 속삭였다. 월남으로 출발할 때 70키로였으니 무려 16키로나 빠졌어. 퍽 장난스런 목소리였다.

his wrist, and left unforgettable words engraved on Ik-su's heart. *Once he has made his choice, a human being should endure and fight in the place where fate has brought him.* By rejecting Capt. Bak's request, Ik-su felt that he had rejected the place to which fate had led him. His fate must have been to stay on in Vietnam and die in the jungle... This regret pierced his mind like an awl even though he was only half conscious.

"Don't lose courage. Why didn't you wake me up?" Suk-hui scolded her husband.

"I'd really, like, to, die, quietly, now."

Mumbling, Ik-su barely finished his sentence.

"Why are you dying? How can you die without even knowing the name or cause of your illness? Wouldn't that be such a shame?"

Yeong-ho didn't move. He looked like someone who had lost consciousness and collapsed.

"I'm not going to the hospital... Never..."

Suk-hui realized that her husband was losing consciousness again. She had to get him to the hospital right away. Moving past Yeong-ho, she went to the phone. According to the wall clock it was two A.M. She had to call a taxi from downtown. She didn't bother calling an ambulance, which had to come

그 밤을 보내고 다섯 달이 지나서 둘은 결혼식을 올렸다. 익수가 약속대로 읍내 장터 근처에 목공소를 차렸다. 손재주가 뛰어난 그는 첫아들을 얻기 직전에 가게를 확장했다. 숙희는 밥 짓고 빨래하고 화장품 바르는 것이 일과의 전부였다. 행복한 3년이 흘렀다. 영호는 돌을 지났다. 뙤약볕이 좋은 어느 여름날이었다. 그늘에서 대패질에 열중하는 익수의 손등, 팔뚝, 얼굴이 갑자기 벌겋게 익어버렸다. 한순간에 '나 병장' 시절의 고통이 되살아난 것이었다. 고약한 피부병 같은 증세를 그는 그해 여름에만 서너 차례를 겪었다. 뾰족한 처방이 없었다. 시간에 맡겨서 스러지기를 기다릴 따름이었다. 통증이 사라지고 피부색이 정상을 회복하면 익수는 늘 웃으며 말했다. 월남에 있을 때도 꼭 이랬는데 시간이 약이더라. 그의 말마따나 번번이 시간이 약이었다. 숙희는 병원에 가자는 채근을 슬며시 접곤 했다.

한사코 병원을 거부해온 익수가 제 발로 병원을 찾아간 것은 1973년이었다. 제대하고 5년을 지난 초여름이었다. 그날 익수는 아내에게 숨이 가빠 못 살겠다는 호소를 했다. 숙희는 남편과 함께 읍내 개인병원을 찾았다.

오십 대 후반의 의사는 엑스레이 사진을 들여다보며 고

from too far away. She was calm. Taking a note from under the telephone, she turned toward the veranda, illuminated by the outside lamp.

The phone was ringing. Once, twice, three times... Suk-hui was getting anxious. *Maybe everyone went home already?* Luckily, a thick voice answered after the seventh ring.

"It's Mr. Kim Ik-su's house in Cape Homi."

"Oh, yes, the defoliant patient."

"It's really urgent. Please come quick! I have to take him to the emergency room."

"He collapsed again? Be prepared. I'll be there like a bullet!"

"Please come up to the empty lot in front of our house. There's nobody in the house who can help me with him."

"OK, I got it."

Putting the receiver down, Suk-hui sighed, relieved. Ik-su was lying there as if dead. Yeong-ho was lying face down as if he was dead, too. Suk-hui gritted her teeth. She turned away from her husband. She turned away from her son, too. Only then did she feel she could prepare herself for going to the hospital.

Suk-hui opened a drawer in the TV table. She

개를 갸우뚱갸우뚱하다가 다짜고짜 익수에게 농사를 많이 짓느냐고 물었다. 부부는 쿡쿡 웃었다. 의사가 눈을 둥그렇게 떴다. 내가 잘못 짚었나요? 숙희가 손을 저었다. 선생님 코에 코딱지가 붙었어요. 의사가 너털웃음을 터뜨리고 휴지로 코를 풀었다. 부부는 긴장을 풀었다. 그러나 의사는 전혀 웃을 기분이 아닌 것 같았다. 똑같은 질문을 처음보다 더 진지하게 물었다. 농사를 많이 짓나요? 익수가 아니라고 했다. 의사가 질문을 고쳤다. 그러면 농약을 많이 취급한 경험이 있나요? 익수는 또 아니라고 했다. 의사가 난처한 표정으로 골똘히 생각하다가 조금은 자신 없는 선고를 내렸다. 그러면 폐결핵일 가능성이 큰데 아주 상태가 심해서 장기간 결핵약을 복용해야 합니다. 익수가 더듬더듬 실토를 했다. 농약은 아니고요, 월남전에 갔다 왔는데, 월남서 독가스를 많이 취급했습니다. 씨에스파우더, 낙엽살초제 같은 것을 자주 다룬 화학병 출신입니다. 의사는 흠칫 놀랐다. 진료비도 안 받을 테니 사실대로만 얘기해 달라고 했다.

의사는 다른 환자들을 대기시키고 무려 한 시간 가까이 익수의 체험담을 경청했다. 답례는 한 바가지 넘는 약봉지였다. 의사가 숙희에게 시아버지처럼 포근히 당부했다.

took out a Medicare card and put her day's wages from the canning factory into her purse. With that money, she wouldn't be kicked out of the emergency room. She took down some clothes that had been hanging from the wall: a pair of baggy jeans randomly chosen at the marketplace and a yellowish green, long-sleeved shirt—a very common outfit for canning factory workers. They didn't smell like fish because they had been laundered. After changing into them, she checked to make sure she hadn't forgotten anything. She caught sight of the chamber pot. *I'd better empty and wash it.* But she stopped short. *Since that reporter said he'd come again, I'd better keep it. He's going to come tomorrow. I should just cover it. If he wants the most miserable sight, then he should have come right now.* Suk-hui was suddenly angry for no reason.

"Kehuh, kehuh."

Suddenly Yeong-ho had dry coughs. Suk-hui waited for his next movement. She thought he would ask her for help with his bodily functions. But he was quiet. He didn't express any concern for his father. He didn't say anything. It was as if he had given a sign that he was alive, just because he was bored. He was looking quietly at the cassette player.

반공법이다 국가보안법이다 해서 그런 하소연을 해볼 자리도 없는데, 어쨌거나 결핵약이라도 끊지 말고 돈 아끼지 말고 맛있는 거 많이 해주세요.

그러나 결핵약은 효험이 없었다. 그때부터 다시 5년이 지났을 즈음, 숙희의 눈을 뒤집는 사태가 벌어졌다. 정겹게 이야기를 나누고 있던 익수가 장난을 하듯이 까무러쳐서 온몸이 뻣뻣해지는 마비를 일으킨 것이었다. 두 달에한 번, 달포에 한 번, 간질병 환자의 발작과 같은 증세는 시간이 흐를수록 서서히 간격이 잦아졌다. 처음 몇 번은 그의 실신이 온 동네를 시끌벅적 뒤흔들었다. 까무러친그를 깨우느라 장정들이 몰려와서 찬물을 퍼부었다. 얼굴을 패기도 했다. 깨어난 그는 입이 아파서 며칠 동안 밥을제대로 씹지도 못했다.

이태가 더 지났다. 뻐꾸기가 우는 날이었다. 낮잠을 자고 있던 익수가 피를 게워내고 읍내 의사에게 실려 갔다. 의사는 시내 종합병원으로 옮기라고 했다. 이듬해였다. 역시 뻐꾸기가 우는 아침이었다. 익수는 또 피를 게워내고 응급실로 실려 갔다. 그것이 해마다 일어났다. 죽음의예행 연습과 같은 연중행사로 굳어졌다. 뻐꾸기가 돌아와울고 있으면 마치 그놈이 몹쓸 병마를 물고 와서 익수의

But Suk-hui decided that she shouldn't waste her energy on her son.

"Ho, I'm not emptying that chamber pot on purpose. I'll take it to the bathroom and keep it covered. If the reporter and the doctor visit by any chance while I'm not home, tell them that's the blood your father vomited. They can do whatever they want with it, take a picture of it, take it and examine it, boil it and eat it. Your father is going to the hospital he always goes to. Got it?"

Yeong-ho moved his jaw up and down. After taking care of the chamber pot, Suk-hui returned to the room. She remembered one thing. She moved the phone within Yeong-ho's reach. She wanted Yeong-ho not to struggle if there was a phone call.

"Ho, if I don't call by the morning, know that your father is fine again. Although it's unlikely, if anything happens to him, I'll give you a call right away." Suk-hui's tone was intentionally serious. She wanted to tell him to please be concerned about his father. Yeong-ho twisted his neck to the right just a little bit and glared at the phone. But he was smiling.

"Father never dies, right? It hasn't been just once or twice that he seemed on the brink of death, but

몸속으로 옮긴 것처럼 그는 반드시 한 번씩 피를 게워내고 응급실로 실려 갔다.

익수는 대패도 톱도 놓아야 했다. 향긋한 나무 냄새와 담을 쌓아야 했다. 그의 가정은, 남편이 돈벌이를 못 할 뿐만 아니라 이따금 병원에 다니면서 돈을 까먹는 가정으로 바뀌었다. 아내가 돈을 벌어야 했다. 병마와 맞서는 남편, 무럭무럭 자라나는 두 아들. 숙희는 해수욕도 싫어했던 몸뚱이 하나를 바다에 팔기로 각오했다. 내 운명이다. 이 한마디를 심장에 새겼다. 읍내의 목공소와 기와집을 팔았다. 익수의 고향 마을인 호미곶으로 돌아가서 움막 같은 집으로 들어갔다. 그리고 십여 년이 흘러갔다. 여자의 몸뚱이 하나로 버티기엔 시골 살림을 탕진할 만한 세월이었다. 두 아들을 공고(工高)로 보낼 수밖에 없었다. 영호마저 기도원으로 보낼 때는 시부모가 물려준 몇 마지기 논밭까지 팔았다. 아직도 호미곶에는 모두가 공유하는 말이 살아 있다. 김익수네 돈 빌려주면 사람 잃고 돈 잃는다.

he got up just fine as if waking from sleep, right? I think he'll revive in a few hours."

Suk-hui was furious. Her face flushed like a flame, because she couldn't spank the bottom of her son who was far too indifferent about his father. She didn't want to see her son or her husband. As if going out to greet the taxi, she went through the front gate. Only then did she bury her face into her hands. She tried hard not to cry. She squatted on the road. This was the very spot where Ik-su waited for the van bringing Yeong-ho home. *When it's hard, remember the good times.* Suk-hui recalled her precept for life that she recited to herself many times each day. It was like a key to the safe where she had hidden some happiness, and about which she was the only person who knew. Recollections and memories... How quickly time flies in those spaces. She could revisit her courtship and honeymoon in a very short time while resting.

*

Suk-hui and Ik-su were from the same village where they met when they were young, and they were going steady before Ik-su enlisted. Suk-hui

숙희가 미소를 머금었다. 읍내에서 오는 택시를 기다리
는 사람이 순간적으로 하얗게 택시를 까먹었다.

"그날 밤을 보자면 적어도 네 개는 있어야지."

가만히 자신에게 속삭인 숙희가 손가락을 하나씩 접었
다. 영화, 보리 냄새, 무덤, 달.

일요일이었다. 둘이서 읍내 극장에 갔다. 저물 무렵에
함께 버스를 타고 동네로 돌아왔다. 익수가 오늘 밤 10시
에 다시 만나자고 했다. 숙희는 가슴이 벌렁거렸다. 그것
은 기묘한 육감이었다. 오늘 밤에 다시 만나면 영원히 기
억할 일이 벌어질 것 같았다. 아까 보았던 미국 영화의 러
브신 같은 장면을 피할 수 없을 것 같았다. 그러나 숙희는
도저히 거절할 수 없었다. 호랑이 꼬리의 꼭짓점 같은 바
위. 익수가 먼저 와서 기다리고 있었다. 일부러 5분쯤 늦
은 숙희에게 그가 말했다. 일제가 국산보다 5분 빠르다.
숙희는 농담이 귀여워서 날름 팔짱을 끼웠다. 익수의 손
목에는 박문현 대위가 선물한 세이코 시계가 걸려 있고,
숙희의 손목에는 그가 선물한 국산 시계가 걸려 있었다.

익수는 해안선을 따라 동네를 벗어나서 방향을 보리밭

opposed his volunteering for the Maengho troops. She said she preferred him to a thousand pieces of gold. But Ik-su didn't listen. He wanted to earn some money in Vietnam so that when he returned home he could set up his own shop and begin his career as a carpenter instead of continuing to work as a mechanic.

Suk-hui regularly sent him a letter, three times a month, and Ik-su usually replied to two of the three. *I love you. I love you, too.* They never skipped those words. These sweet professions of love through letters nurtured their love, although they felt shy using those same words face-to-face, even after they married.

The day Ik-su returned to the port of Busan, Suk-hui went to welcome him. He looked different. His face was flushed like a strawberry, and he looked slimmer. But she was simply glad and moved. There was no time for her to be sensitive to those changes. She just thought he looked different because he had been exposed to the sun and sweated a lot.

Ik-su returned home in March, 1968 and was discharged in April. He weighed only 54kg. A fortnight later, on a moonlit night when the barley field in

쪽으로 돌렸다. 그 유혹이 숙희는 싫지 않았다. 밤새 걸어
보자는 말로 시침을 뗐을 뿐이었다. 비스듬한 오르막길이
지만 직선으로 걸어가면 10분도 안 걸릴 보리밭 횡단에
두 사람은 한 시간을 더 바쳤다. 쉰 자죽을 옮기면 5분을
멈춰서 입맞춤에 열중했던 것이다. 보리밭의 위쪽과 솔밭
이 맞닿는 한 지점에 낮은 무덤이 있었다.

숙희가 파뿌리 같은 귀밑머리를 두 손으로 쓸었다. 그 무
덤에 닿자 새삼 쑥스러웠다. 황홀한 손길. 살을 찢는 고통.
짜릿짜릿한 전율의 반복. 깨무는 신음 소리…… 사랑하는
이를 최초로 받아들였다는 뿌듯한 성취감과 뜨거운 희열.

"그날 밤 그 달은 어디로 갔나."

숙희가 두리번두리번 하늘을 쳐다보았다. 그날 밤에 무
덤가의 사랑을 내려다보았던 그 살진 달은 보이지 않았
다. 박꽃처럼 창백한 별들만 촘촘했다.

보리밭 사이로 내려오는 길에 익수는 숙희를 업었다.
평생 이렇게 업고 살 거니까 올해 가을에는 식 올리자. 숙
희는 눈물이 핑 돌았다. 그가 노래를 한 곡씩만 부르자고
했다. 당신이 먼저 불러요. 숙희는 자신도 모르게 '당신'
이라 했다. 익수가 숙희를 내려서 입맞춤을 했다. 길었다.
긴 입맞춤이 끝났을 때, 숙희가 말했다. 만약 사랑하는 두

Cape Homi was turning golden, Ik-su and Suk-hui made love. At that time he whispered to Suk-hui, *I lost as much as 16kg, since I weighed 70kg when I left for Vietnam.* He sounded playful.

They had their wedding five months after that night. Ik-su opened a carpenter's shop near the downtown marketplace, as he planned. An exceptionally handy man, he expanded his shop right before the birth to their first son. Suk-hui's daily schedule consisted of cooking, laundering, and putting on make-up. Three happy years passed. They had just celebrated Yeong-ho's first birthday. One sunny summer morning, the backs of Ik-su's hands, his arms and face suddenly became flushed while he was absorbed in planning some wood. The pain he had experienced as "Sgt. Na" abruptly returned. These symptoms, like those of a nasty skin disease, returned three or four times that summer. There was no easy cure. Ik-su had to wait for them to disappear on their own. After the pains were gone and his skin had regained its normal color, he always said, with a smile, *This happened in Vietnam, too. Time was the only cure.* As he said, time always cured him. Suk-hui gradually stopped urging him to go to the hospital.

167

사람이 하루의 절반을 입맞춤에 쓴다면 그 시간이 보통 시간보다 두 배나 빨리 흐르기 때문에 두 사람의 수명이 그만큼 줄어들 것 같아요. 익수가 한 번 더 억센 키스를 하고 다시 숙희를 업었다.

노래는 익수가 먼저 불렀다. 베트남에서 오는 편지가 가끔 혼자서 흥얼거린다고 썼던 그 노래였다. 남쪽 나라 십자성은 어머님 얼굴, 눈에 익은 너의 모습 꿈속에 보면, 꽃이 피고 새가 우는 바닷가 저편에, 고향 산천 가는 길이 고향 산천 가는 길이 절로 열리네.

"당신은 애달프게 불렀지……. 나는 더 애달프게 불렀지."

숙희가 예쁘게 웃었다. 그날 밤에 불렀던 자기 노래에 변함없이 높은 점수를 매긴 것이었다. 베트남으로 보내는 편지가 혼자서 자주 부른다고 썼던 그 노래였다.

헤일 수 없이 수많은 밤을
내 가슴 도려내는 아픔에 겨워
얼마나 울었던가 동백 아가씨
그리움에 지쳐서 울다 지쳐서
꽃잎은 빨갛게 멍이 들었네.

In 1973, however, Ik-su volunteered to go to the hospital, which he had previously refused to do. In the early summer five years after his discharge, Ik-su complained to his wife about being short of breath. Suk-hui and Ik-su went to a small clinic downtown.

The doctor, in his fifties, was tilting his head left and right in front of the X-ray film and abruptly asked Ik-su if he did a lot of farming. The couple giggled. The doctor's eyes grew bigger. *I guessed wrong?* Suk-hui waved her hand. *You have dried mucus hanging from your nose.* Laughing loudly, the doctor blew his nose on a piece of tissue paper. The couple relaxed. But the doctor didn't look in the mood for smiles. He repeated the same question, only much more seriously this time. *Are you farming a lot?* Ik-su said *no.* The doctor revised his question. *Then, have you handled agrichemicals a lot?* Ik-su denied this again. The doctor was thinking hard, his expression suggesting that he was at a loss, and then he declared, without confidence. *If that's the case, then this could be tuberculosis. It's very serious, so you have to take an anti-tuberculosis drug for a long time.* Ik-su stammered to confess, *I didn't handle agrichemicals, but I've been to*

그날 밤에 '동백 아가씨'를 부르는 사람은 몰랐지만 듣는 사람은 영혼이 뭉클했다. 혼자서 자주 부른다던 이 노래가 실은 숙희의 속살을 도려내는 노래였구나. 연장 근무 안 하기를 잘 했지. 박 대위에게 넘어갔으면 또 얼마나 숙희가 가슴을 도려내게 만들었겠는가. 남쪽 나라의 전쟁터에 나가 있는 임을 그리워하면서 임의 무사귀환을 앙망해온 갯가 처녀의 곡진한 소망이 드디어 갯가 청년의 무딘 가슴을 징처럼 울리고 있었다.

"엄마, 저 새는 이름이 뭐야?"

"뻐꾸기."

"뻐꾹 뻐꾹 운다고 뻐꾸기야?

"그래."

어린 영호와 나눈 대화였다. 무슨 실수처럼 그것이 고막을 건드리자 숙희는 소름이 돋았다. 익수가 처음 피를 토한 한낮이 바로 그날이었다. 갑자기 엔진 소리가 밤의 정적을 깨고 있다. 택시가 골목으로 올라오는 것이다. 숙희가 어금니를 물고 일어섰다. 택시의 불빛이 쪽마루에 시신처럼 드러누운 익수를 비출 때, 엉덩이를 툭툭 터는 숙희의 모습이 달콤한 휴식시간을 마치고 작업장으로 복귀하려는 노동자 같다.

Vietnam, where I handled a lot of poisonous gas. I was a chemical specialist and I handled CS powder and defoliants often. Surprised, the doctor shrank back a little. Saying that he wouldn't charge his usual fee, he asked Ik-su to tell him exactly what he did and experienced.

Running far behind schedule, the doctor intently listened to Ik-su's story for almost an hour. He rewarded Ik-su with a bag full of pills, more than a gourd full. The doctor warmly begged Suk-hui as if he were her father-in-law. *The Anti-communism Law and National Security Law make it really impossible to appeal anywhere about this. At any rate, please don't let him stop taking the anti-tuberculosis drug and cook him lots of delicious food, sparing no expense.*

But the anti-tuberculosis drug was no help at all. About five years later an incident that greatly upset Suk-hui happened. In the middle of a loving conversation, Ik-su fainted and his body suddenly became stiff, as if he was joking around. As time passed, he had an epileptic fit more and more often, at first once every other month, and then about once a month. The first few times, his convulsion shocked the entire neighborhood. In order to

어둠, 적막, 혼자.

세 단어의 현실적 성립이 영호는 마음에 들었다.

아랫방이 비었다. 동생이 집에 없다.

그 조건이 그는 흡족했다.

"불 꺼주고 가라!"

아버지를 안고 나가는 택시 기사를 좇아가는 어머니의 등에다 내질렀던 고함. 그것은 아주 마음에 들었다. 뒤늦게 쾌재를 부르고 싶었다.

영호가 빙긋이 웃었다. 하지만 그것은 달랐다. 익수가 징그럽게 느낀 달관의 것이 아니었다. 은밀히 추진해온 음모를 성공한 자가 남몰래 짓는 음흉스런 회심의 웃음, 그런 것이었다.

복음기도원을 출발하기 전에 영호는 집에서 지킬 3대 수칙을 정했다. 싸늘하게, 무뚝뚝하게, 때로는 달관한 도인처럼. 그는 아버지와 어머니에게 보여준 자기 태도와 표정과 말투를 찬찬히 돌이켜보았다. 3대 수칙을 철저히 지킨 것 같았다. 그만큼 몹쓸 자식으로 굴었다. 이 사실을 그는 장한 일로 받아들였다.

wake him up, vigorous men gathered and poured cold water on him. Sometimes, they tried slapping his face. After he woke up, he couldn't chew food for a few days because his mouth hurt.

Two years passed. On a day when the cuckoos were crying, Ik-su vomited blood in the middle of a nap and was rushed to a downtown clinic. The doctor told him to go to the main hospital in the nearby city. The next year, again on a day when the cuckoos were crying, Ik-su vomited blood and was rushed to the emergency room. The same thing happened every year. This event, like rehearsal for death, became an annual ritual. Whenever the cuckoos returned to cry, it seemed that they drove a ghastly curse of disease into Ik-su's body, and he ended up vomiting blood and being taken to the emergency room.

Ik-su had to give up his plane and saw. He had to forget the faint, sweet smell of wood. In his family, the head of the household not only earned no money but also occasionally squandered it at the hospital. His wife had to make the money. With a husband fighting the demon of disease and two rapidly growing young sons, Suk-hui decided to sell her body—a body that had disliked even sea

그러나 아직은 남은 일이 있었다. 아버지와 어머니, 아니, 아버지였다. 그는 어머니의 품에 영섭을 맡겼다. 어머니의 품에는 동생이 있어야 하고, 동생의 품에는 어머니가 있어야 한다. 나를 어머니의 품에서 분리시켜야 한다. 이 의식을 확고히 했다. 그는 자신을 아버지의 품에 맡기고 아버지를 자신의 품에 안았다. 아버지의 품에 내가 있어야 하고, 내 품에 아버지가 있어야 한다. 이 의식도 확고히 했다. 이제부터 그는 아버지를 넘으려 했다. 뉴스에 나온 어머니의 절규에서는 아버지가 죽음도 비켜가는 밥벌레였지만, 하반신 못 쓰는 아들에게는 아버지가 존재 영역을 한정짓는 그물이었다.

아버지를 의식한 영호가 전화통으로 시선을 옮겨갔다. 그것은 옥색을 낡은 야광 물체처럼 머금고 있었다. 그가 오래 전화통을 응시했다. 전화통이 겁을 집어먹고 따르릉 따르릉 비명을 지를 때까지 최면을 거는 것 같았다.

빙긋이, 영호가 웃음을 지었다. 아버지에게 보여준 그 웃음이었다. 삼라만상에 무심한 듯한, 세상만사에 달관한 듯한. 문득 그 웃음을 거울에서 한번 만나고 싶었다. 지난 봄날을 꼬박 바쳐서 수없이 연습한, 겸손과 오만이 절묘하게 궁합을 맞춘 것이라고 믿었던 웃음. 그러나 당장은

bathing—to the sea. *This is my fate.* She inscribed those words deep in her heart. They sold their tile-roofed house and Ik-su's woodworking shop downtown. Returning to Cape Homi, their home village, they began living in a small house that resembled a mud hut. Ten years had passed since then. It was time enough to run through all their assets, even while living in that tiny country house. A woman's body wasn't sufficient to sustain it. They had to send their two sons to a technical high school. When they had to send Yeong-ho to the prayer house, they had to sell the last few small plots of rice paddies they inherited from Ik-su's parents. There was a saying in Cape Homi that everyone knew: If you lend money to Kim Ik-su's family, you lose both your friend and your money.

*

Suk-hui smiled. She completely forgot that she was waiting for a taxi from downtown.

"I need at least four fingers to think about that night." Quietly murmuring to herself, Suk-hui began folding her fingers one by one: the movie, the smell of barley, the grave, and the moon.

확인할 방법이 없었다. 거울은 벽에 걸려 있었다. 그 점이 괜히 억울했다. 죽는 날까지 절대 거울을 안 보겠다고 결심한 자가 거울을 볼 수 없는 처지에 대해 분통을 터뜨리려 했다.

영호는 분풀이하는 눈초리로 다시 전화통을 쏘아보았다. 그러나 빙긋이 웃고 말았다. 이번에는 냉소에 가까웠다. 숱한 시간을 바쳐서 간신히 터득한 그 웃음을 스스로 우스갯거리로 만들 뻔했던 자기 성깔에게 보낸 것이었다.

영호가 두 팔을 위로 뻗고 얼굴을 숙였다. 이마와 코가 바닥에 닿았다. 주먹을 불끈 쥐었다. 집에 다니러 가겠다고 결심한 그때의 소망이 오롯이 손에 잡히는 듯했다.

"아버지, 이번에는 그만……. 저는 포기한 게 아닙니다."

영호가 해골 같은 아버지의 얼굴을 그리며 기도하듯 중얼거렸다. 눈가에는 눈물이 맺히고 있었다. 그는 손을 뻗어 녹음기 밑에서 종이를 빼냈다. 절반으로 접힌 하얀 종이였다. 그것을 펼쳤다. 그가 '인간 선언'이라는 제목을 붙인 글이다. 육필이다. 어둠 속에서도 그는 읽을 수 있다.

이 세계가 나에게 안긴 최악의 선물은 폭력이며,

One Sunday, they went to the downtown theatre together. They came back to their village by bus. Ik-su asked her to meet him again at 10 P.M. Suk-hui's heart was pounding. Somehow she instinctively knew that something unforgettable would happen if she met him that night. It seemed that they couldn't avoid a love scene like the one in the film they had just watched. Even though Suk-hui was aware of this, she couldn't refuse. Ik-su was waiting for her at the rock like the tip of the tiger's tail, when she arrived. He said to Suk-hui, who was intentionally five minutes late, *the Japanese watch is five minutes faster than the Korean watch*. Finding his joke cute, she immediately linked her arm with his. Ik-su was wearing the Seiko watch Capt. Bak Mun-hyeon had given him, and Suk-hui was wearing the Korean watch Ik-su had given her.

Ik-su led the way along the beach out of the village toward the barley fields. Suk-hui didn't mind that he was seducing her. She simply feigned ignorance, proposing that they'd walk all night. They spent more than an hour crossing the barley field. It was a gentle upward slope, and it would have taken them less than ten minutes if they had walked straight across. But they kept on kissing for five

이 세계가 나에게 남긴 최선의 선물은 분노이다.
내 하반신에 엉켜 사라지지 않는 폭력에 대한 분노를
더 참을 수 없어 이 세계로 돌려주는 그 순간,
마침내 나는 영원히 온전한 인간을 회복한다.

오래 묵상에 잠겼던 영호가 요 밑에 오른손을 넣었다. 티끌 같은 두려움도 없는 동작이었다. 있었다. 잘 있었다. 정갈한 손이 오기를 기다리고 있었다. 그는 그것을 힘껏 움켜쥐었다. 배꼽 부위에서 치솟은 전율이 정수리를 쿡 쑤셨다. 눈앞에 별빛 조각들이 튀었다. 아찔한 환희였다.

영호는 요 밑의 그것을 움켜쥔 그대로 눈을 감았다. 여자 얼굴 하나를 떠올리고 싶었다. 누구든 어머니만 아니면 좋다고 생각했다.

소꿉친구들……

초등학생 때 한 반 계집애들……

중학 시절의 소녀들……

고등학생 때 버스 안에서 눈길을 마주친 여고생들…….

노동자 시절에 본 여사원들…….

그러나 영호는 실패하고 말았다. 단 하나의 또렷한 얼굴을 포착하지 못했다. 기껏 둘이나 셋이 겹쳐지고, 대개

minutes every fifty steps. There was a low grave at the border between the upper end of the barley field and the pine forest above.

Suk-hui brushed her scallion root-like hair behind her ears. When they arrived at the grave, she felt awkward again. Ecstatic touches, skin-tearing pain, a repeated feeling of exhilaration and trembling, the biting sound of moaning... a great sense of ecstasy and achievement from accepting her lover for the first time.

"Where has the moon of that day gone?"

Suk-hui looked up and around the sky. There was no plump moon looking down on love at the grave. Only pale stars densely covered the sky like gourd flowers.

Ik-su piggybacked Suk-hui on their way down across the barley field. *I promise to piggyback you like this forever. Let's get married this fall.* Suk-hui was tearing up. Ik-su proposed that they each sing a song. *You sing first, dear.* She called him "dear" unawares. Ik-su put her down and they kissed. It was a very long kiss. After that long kiss, Suk-hui said, *if lovers spend half their days in kissing, their lifespan will be halved, since the time passes two times more quickly when they kiss.* Ik-su forcefully

군상으로 어른대다가 스러져갔다. 잠깐 외톨로 가물거린 얼굴이 있긴 있었다. 신입사원 시절이었다. 선배들이 막 무가내로 몰아붙였다. 우리 회사는 병역면제라는 엄청난 특혜를 받는 회사니까 입영전야의 환송식이란 게 없는데, 대신에 바로 오늘 같은 저녁을 입영전야처럼 대접해주는 거야. 어처구니없게도 총각딱지를 없애준다는 것이었다. 선배들이 강제로 붙여준 접대부 아가씨. 같이 모텔에 들긴 했으나 몇 분 만에 그냥 돌려보낸 동갑내기. 차라리 돈이 선물한 아가씨의 알몸을 정성껏 품었더라면 지금 그 얼굴이 눈앞에 다정스레 웃고 있을지 몰랐다.

"떠오르는 여자 하나 없구나."

영호가 나직이 속삭였다. 설움은 아니었다. 철강공단 노동자 생활 2년. 병역면제 특혜를 위한 의무기간도 덜 채운 그 2년이 사회생활의 전부였다. 홀가분했다. 그러나 그는 잊은 적이 없었다. 자신의 마비된 하반신 속에는 이 세계가 개인 김영호에게 일방적으로 맺은 관계의 전부가 엉켜 있다는 점을 명백히 기억하고 있었다.

kissed Suk-hui again, and then piggybacked her again.

Ik-su sang first. It was the song he had mentioned singing occasionally in a letter from Vietnam. *Northern Cross from a southern country is Mother's face/ when I see your familiar face in my dream/ across the seashore where flowers bloom and birds sing/ the way to my homeland, the way to my homeland opens up on its own.*

"You sang so sadly... and I sang even more sadly."

Suk-hui smiled prettily. She never failed to think highly of her own singing that night. She sang the song she mentioned often singing by herself in her letter to Vietnam.

How much you've cried, dear Miss Camellia,
Overwhelmed by heart-wrenching sorrows
On innumerable nights!
Exhausted from longing,
Exhausted from crying,
Petals are bruised crimson red.

The singer who sang the song "Miss Camellia" that night didn't know how deeply it moved the soul of its listener. *This song she mentioned singing often*

*

선잠인 듯 꿈결인 듯 영호가 비몽사몽 의식을 놓친 뒤에도 초여름 짧은 밤은 어김없이 제 시간을 운행하여 이윽고 수평선 아래에서 붉은 기운이 우러나고 있었다. 어쩌면 보리밭 너머 뒷산의 뻐꾸기도 날개를 털고 있을 즈음이었다. 그는 엎드린 그대로 왼쪽 귀를 바닥에 대고 가늘게 코를 골고 있었다.

영호가 두세 차례 마른기침을 했다. 수평선에는 선홍빛 해가 이마를 내미는 참이었다.

"따르릉, 따르릉."

움찔 놀란 영호가 고개를 세웠다.

"따르릉, 따르릉."

환청인가 꿈속인가. 그가 눈을 똑바로 떴다.

"따르릉, 따르릉."

분명히 옥색 전화통이 머리맡에서 울고 있었다. 그는 받지 않았다. 자꾸만 따르릉거렸다. 기어이 잠든 자를 깨우겠다는 작정 같았다. 한 번 시작한 뻐꾸기의 울음만큼 길어질지는 기다려봐야 알 테지만.

"따르릉, 따르릉, 따르릉, 따르릉."

was in fact a song that thoroughly broke her heart!
I'm so glad I didn't volunteer to extend my duty in
Vietnam. If I took Capt. Bak's bait, how much more
heartbreak I would have caused Suk-hui! The heart-
felt wish of a fishing village girl for the safe return
of her dearly missed lover from the battlegrounds of
a southern country was resounding like a gong in
the simple heart of a young man from the fishing
village.

"Mom, what's the name of that bird?"

"Cuckoo."

"Because it's crying cuckoo, cuckoo?"

"That's right."

She talked like that with young Yeong-ho. When
that conversation touched her eardrums like a mis-
take, Suk-hui got goose bumps. She had that conversation on the very afternoon when Ik-su vomited
blood for the first time. Suddenly the sound of an
engine shattered the night's quiet. The taxi was
climbing up the alley. Gritting her teeth, Suk-hui
stood up. When the headlights of the taxi fell on Ik-
su, lying like a dead body on the narrow veranda,
Suk-hui looked like a laborer returning to work
after a sweet rest, dusting off her pants.

영호가 숨을 멈췄다.

"아버지, 고맙습니다. 오늘 이 아침에 온전한 인간을 회복하겠습니다."

전화를 받은 것처럼 말한 영호가 빙긋이 웃었다. 삼라만상에 무심하고 세상만사에 달관한 것이라고 자부하는 웃음이었다.

"따르릉."

그가 요 밑으로 오른손을 넣었다 잽싸게 빼내고 왼쪽 손목을 턱 앞으로 당겼다.

"따르릉."

불끈, 그가 왼손으로 주먹을 쥐었다. 몇 가닥의 핏줄이 전선처럼 불거졌다. 여전히 그는 빙긋이 웃고 있었다.

"딱. 딱. 딱."

손톱을 다듬던 칼이 딱딱한 소리로 날카로운 날을 드러냈다. 영호는 주저하지 않았다. 죽음의 이빨 같은 그것으로 즉시 왼쪽 손목의 핏줄 하나를 겨누었다. 쿡! 배꼽에서 치솟은 전율이 정수리를 쑤셨다. 그 아찔한 환희의 힘을 그는 고스란히 오른손으로 이동시켰다.

"……따르릉, 따르릉, 따르릉."

뻐꾸기 대신 울고 있던 전화통이 뚝 그쳤다. 녹음기 앞

*

Darkness, silence, solitude.

Yeong-ho liked the actualization of these three words.

The other room was empty. His brother was not home.

He liked it.

"Please turn off the light before you leave!" he yelled after his mother who was following the taxi driver who was carrying his father. He liked it very much. Belatedly, he wanted to cry out "bravo!"

Yeong-ho smiled. This smile was different from the sage-like smile Ik-su found creepy. It was the wicked smile of a self-satisfied person who had succeeded in accomplishing a secret mission he had been working on for some time.

Before he left the Gospel Prayer House, Yeong-ho decided that he would stick to three principles at home: Behave coldly, behave brusquely, and sometimes behave like a sage! He reflected slowly on his own attitudes, expressions, and manners of speaking. He felt that he had strictly adhered to his resolution. Therefore he had behaved like an ingrate. He thought it a great achievement.

의 절반으로 접힌 하얀 종이가 모서리부터 붉게 물들고 있었다. 하반신이 마비된 한 젊은이가 이 세계를 상대로 쓴 짤막한 글이 바로 자신의 피에 젖는 중이었다.

슬로우 불릿, 아시아, 2013

But he had one more task to finish. It was his parents, no, his father. He decided to leave Yeong-seop to the care of his mother. *My mother has to embrace my brother and my brother has to embrace my mother. I have to separate myself from my mother.* He firmly told himself this. He entrusted his father with himself and embraced him. *My father has to embrace me and I have to embrace my father.* He firmly told himself this, too. From now on he wanted to supersede his father. Although his father was a "useless mouth that even death avoided" according to his mother's desperate cry, to him, paralyzed from the waist down, he was a net confining his whole being.

Thinking of his father, Yeong-ho glanced at the telephone. It held its light blue color like an old glow-in-the-dark object. He stared at the phone for a long time. It was as if he was hypnotizing the phone until it became so scared that it would eventually scream, *ting a ling, ting a ling.*

Yeong-ho gently smiled. It was the same smile that he showed his father, a smile that seemed indifferent to the universe, a smile above the business of the world. Suddenly he wanted to see his own smile. He devoted all his spring days to practicing that smile, a smile he believed to be an exquisite mixture of humility and arrogance. But right now he couldn't check his smile. The mirror was hanging on the wall. He felt quite upset about this. The person who had decided that he would never look in the mirror until the day he died was about to burst with rage because he couldn't see himself in the mirror.

With indignant, angry eyes, Yeong-ho glared at the telephone again. But he smiled again. This time it was more like a sneer. He was sneering at his own sharp temper that had almost turned his hard-won smile, a smile that took a lot of time to achieve, into mere drollery.

Stretching his arms upward, Yeong-ho lowered his face. His forehead and nose touched the floor. He abruptly made fists. In that moment he felt as if he were fully grasping the wish he had when he decided to visit home.

"Father, this time, please let go... It's not because I'm giving up."

Picturing the skeletal face of his father, Yeong-ho muttered this as if praying. He was tearing up. He reached under the cassette player and took out a piece of paper, a piece of white paper folded in half. He unfolded it. It was entitled "Declaration of a Human Being." It was handwritten. He could read it even in the dark.

The worst gift this world gave me is violence,
The best gift this world gave me is anger.
The moment I return to the world, unable to stand any longer,
my anger toward the violence that wouldn't leave my lower body where it lodged itself,
I finally and eternally reclaim my full humanity.

After a long meditation, Yeong-ho put his right hand under the mattress. There wasn't one iota of fear in his movement. There it was. It was there just fine. It was waiting for a clean hand. He grabbed it tight. A shudder went through his body, soaring from his navel to the crown of his head, which it stabbed. Fragments of stars were sputtering in front of his eyes. It was dizzyingly ecstatic.

Still grabbing it with his hand, Yeong-ho closed his eyes. He wanted to picture the face of a woman. Except for his mother, any woman would do.

Childhood friends...

Young girls in the same elementary school class...

Girls in his middle school days...

High school girls he was eyeing on in the buses in high school...

Female office workers while he was working at the factory...

But he failed. He couldn't picture a single clear face. At best, two or three faces would overlap, then vanish together after lingering awhile. One face flickered by itself for a moment. When he was a new hire, his superiors ruthlessly insisted, *You have no official farewell party before beginning compulsory military service, because our employees are exempt. So tonight we're going to treat you to that kind of party.* Crazily, they insisted that they would help him get rid of his virginity. Older fellows at the company forced him into a motel with an entertainment girl. Although he went to the motel room with her, he sent her away after a few minutes. If he had made love to her, naked, then, he might have had a face smiling affectionately at him at this moment.

"I cannot picture even a single woman." Yeong-ho muttered in a low voice.

He wasn't sad. He worked for two years as a laborer at a steel company. Only two years—he couldn't even fulfill the time requirement for those exempt from compulsory military service. He felt lighthearted. But he never forgot, he clearly remembered, that all the relationships this world had unilaterally with the individual, Kim Yeong-ho, were tangled in his paralyzed lower body.

*

Even after Yeong-ho lost consciousness, maybe in a slumber or maybe in a dream, the short early summer night did not fail to continue to work its way toward dawn when finally a reddish color was beginning to rise from below the horizon. Perhaps the cuckoos on the hills beyond the barley field behind the house were shaking their wings at that very moment. Yeong-ho was snoring lightly, his left ear on the floor, still lying face down.

He gave a few dry coughs. On the horizon, the scarlet sun was pushing its forehead upward.

"Ting a ling, ting a ling."

With a start, Yeong-ho raised his head.

"Ting a ling, ting a ling."

Is this an hallucination or a dream? He opened his eyes wide.

"Ting a ling, ting a ling."

It was clearly the light blue telephone near his head that was ringing. He didn't pick it up. The phone kept on ringing. It seemed determined to wake him no matter what. Whether it lingered as the cuckoo's cries, which lasted very long once they started—remained to be seen.

"Ting a ling, ting a ling, ting a ling, ting a ling."

Yeong-ho stopped breathing.

"Thank you, Father. Today, this morning, I'll resuscitate my full humanity."

After saying like this as if talking on the phone, Yeong-ho smiled. It was that smile he felt proud of because it showed his indifference to the universe and his wisdom as a wise man overcoming all worldly concerns.

"Ting a ling."

He pushed his right hand under the mattress and quickly took it out, and then he pulled his left wrist toward his jaw.

"Ting a ling."

Suddenly and forcefully, he made a fist with his left hand. A few blood vessels bulged out. He was still smiling.

"Tok, tok, tok."

The knife he had used to trim his nails showed its

sharp blade, following a succession of dull noises. Yeong-ho didn't hesitate. He aimed at his wrist with the blad like the fang of death. *Kuk!* A shudder shot from his navel through his entire body to the crown of his head. He shifted all the power of his dizzy ecstasy to his right hand.

"...ting a ling, ting a ling, ting a ling."

The phone that had been crying instead of the cuckoos stopped ringing. The white paper, folded in half and lying in front of the cassette player, was being dyed red, starting with one corner. A short note written to the world by a young man paralyzed from the waist down was being soaked with his own blood.

Translated by Jeon Seung-hee

해설

Afterword

역사적 운명의 탐구, 가려진 진실의 재현

방민호(문학평론가)

　나는 『슬로우 불릿』의 작가 이대환을 비교적 잘 아는 평론가일 것이다. 그는 독특한 이력을 가진 작가다. 1958년생, 포항 영일만에서 출생한 그는 방황 많은 고등학교 시대를 보내고 중앙대학교 문예창작학과에 들어가 김동리, 서정주 등의 지도를 받으며 문학 수업 과정을 거쳤다. 일찍이 서정주에게 시적 재능을 인정받았던 그는 처음에 시를 썼으나 우여곡절 끝에 결국 세상에는 작가로 나왔다.

　그의 삶은 고향인 포항과 뗄 수 없는 관계를 맺어왔다. 대학을 졸업한 그는 고향인 포항에 내려가 국어교사로 재직했으며, 교육 민주화와 관련된 활동을 벌이면서 교사직에서 떠나 오랫동안 지역사회운동을 하게 됐다. 그의 20

Exploring Historical Destiny, Representing Hidden Truths

Bang Min-ho (literary critic)

I know Lee Dae-hwan, the author of *Slow Bullet*, very well. He has had a long, unique career. He was born at Yong-il Bay in Pohang in 1958. He lived there throughout his childhood and tumultuous teen years. Upon graduating high school, he left and studied at the Department of Creative Writing at Choong-Ang University under such masters as Kim Dong-ri and Seo Jeong-ju. After Seo Jeong-ju recognized his poetic talent early on, he began writing poetry. Eventually, though, he debuted as a writer of short stories and fiction.

Since the beginning, Lee's life has been inseparable from his hometown in Pohang. After graduating

대 말 30대 전반기는 1980년대였다. 이 때 한국 사회는 민주화운동의 몸살을 앓았다. 그의 작가로서의 성장과정은 이 시대적 분위기 속에서 이루어졌다.

그는 포스코, 곧 포항제철이 들어서면서 공업도시로 변모해 간 고향에 깊은 애착을 품었다. 나는 이것이 아마도 일종의 실향민 감각일지도 모른다고 생각한다. 그윽한 만과 앙증맞게 바다를 향해 튀어나간 곶이 이루는 목가적 풍경이 어느 날 갑자기 들어서기 시작한 공장 풍경으로 바뀔 때 그 상실감은 합리적이라기보다는 다분히 감성적인 것이었으리라 상상해 볼 수 있다. 1980년대의 민주화운동, 지역사회와 제3세계에 대한 관심이 지극히 정서적인 추동력을 기반으로 삼은 것이었다고도 말할 수 있다면 작가 이대환의 작가적 성장 과정은 고향의 변화가 주는 충격을 수용하는 데 바쳐졌다고도 말할 수 있다.

그는 집념을 품은 작가이며 동시에 이상주의적인 타입의 작가이기도 하다. 교육 민주화에 대한 관심, 포항 사회에 대한 관심은 자연스럽게 그의 소설 세계의 저층을 이루게 된다. 『조그만 깃발 하나』(1995), 『생선 창자 속으로 들어간 詩』(1997)와 같은 창작집에 수록된 중단편소설들 중에는 이러한 작가적 특질이 투영된 것들이 많다.

from college, he returned to Pohang and began work as a Korean teacher. He left his teaching position after he became involved in the democratization movement for education. Throughout his late twenties and early thirties, he became even more involved in the local democratization movement of the 1980s. It was in this general setting that Lee began to mature as a writer.

Lee has always cared deeply for his hometown in Pohang. Pohang, once a remote fishing village, transformed into an industrial city after the foundation of POSCO, the Pohang Steel Company. His feelings regarding the transformation were similar to the dispossessed people in general. When the factory scene replaced the pastoral landscape, the deep, concave bays and the sheer cliffs jutting out over the sea, one can imagine the deep sense of loss Lee and the other villagers of Pohang felt. The democratization movement, interests in local societies and the third world during the 1980s were deeply emotional. Lee's maturation as a writer was also devoted to his adjustment to the shock he felt from the transformation of his hometown.

Lee is an idealistic and uncompromising author. His interest in the democratization of the Korean

그런데 그는 중단편소설의 형식으로는 충분히 감당할 수 없는 소재, 주제들로 관심 지평을 확장시켜 왔다. 『겨울의 집』(1999), 『슬로우 불릿』(2001), 『붉은 고래』(2004) 등의 장편소설들이 그 소산이다. 이 작품들에서 그는 일제 강점기부터 현대에 이르는 가족사를 다루고, 고엽제 후유증을 앓고 있는 베트남 참전 병사 가족의 이야기를 쓰고, 삼형제가 한반도의 서로 다른 운명을 상징하는 길을 걷게 된 사연을 그렸다. 이것은 그가 본질적으로 말해 인간의 삶이 역사와 만나는 장경에 관심을 가진 작가임을 말해준다.

나는 일찍부터 자신이 생각하는 문제들을 외면하지 않고 직격해 들어가는 이 작가의 스타일에 관심을 품었다. 이러한 그의 성향은 자신의 문제의식을 1980년대라는 시대의 한계에 가둬두지 않는 것으로 나타난다. 그는 더 넓고 깊은 관점에서 생각하게 되는 것, 더 진실하다고 생각하게 되는 것을 외면하지 않고 자신의 문제로 받아들이는 태도를 견지해 왔다고 말할 수 있다. 포항에 철강왕국을 이루는 박태준 씨(평전 『박태준』, 2004)나 북한 체제를 평가하는(장편소설 『큰돈과 콘돔』, 2009) 그의 관점에 이러한 태도가 배여 있어서, 나는 이것이 작가적 진정성에 관계하

educational system and the city of Pohang was the foundation for his fiction. Many of his stories and novellas in *A Small Flag* (1995) and *Poems That Ended up in the Intestines of Fish* (1997) reflect these deep sentiments.

Lee gradually expanded the scope of his interests to include stories that could not be dealt within the frameworks of the short story and the novella. Novels like *House of Winter* (1999), *Slow Bullet* (2001), and *Red Whale* (2004) were the result of his new artistic direction. In these novels, he dealt with entirely different subject matters: the history of a family from the Japanese colonial period to the present day, a Vietnam War veteran's family's struggle with the aftereffects of chemical warfare, and the branching fates and directions of the Korean Peninsula, as represented by the branching fates and directions of three Korean brothers. These stories suggest that Lee is an author interested in the points of contact between history and life.

I am deeply impressed by Lee's straightforward approach to the problems that drew his interest. This approach is embodied in his refusal to limit his interests only to the conflicts of the 1980s. He has consistently tackled issues head-on as his knowl-

는 것이라 생각하고 있다.

세계 현대사의 진로를 규정한 냉전체제가 사람들의 삶에 미치는 영향을 특정한 이데올로기적 관점을 넘어서서 더 근본적으로 해부하고자 하는 그의 태도는 이 시대를 헤쳐 나오고 또 이 시대에 의해 희생된 이들의 운명을 형상화하는 쪽으로 표현되었다. 그 결과 작가로서 그는 운명적으로 역사에 연루될 수밖에 없었던 이들의 생애, 그들의 심리를 묘파해내는 데 특별한 능력을 발휘한다. 『슬로우 불릿』은 그 단적인 예에 해당하는 작품이다.

『슬로우 불릿』은 일반 독자들에게 널리 알려지지 않았다. 그러나 이 작품을 접한 독자들은 주제와 분량의 조화, 완벽한 플롯, 작가가 제시하는 역사적 비극에 깊은 공감을 표현하기를 주저하지 않았다. 인터넷을 통해서 이를 확인해 볼 수 있다.

이 소설의 제목인 '슬로우 불릿'이라는 말은 고엽제 환자가 처한 상황을 단적으로 드러내는 말이다. 고엽제 환자들, 즉 베트남 전쟁 때 미군이 베트남 지역에 살포한 고엽제에 노출된 후유증을 앓는 환자들은 자신을 서서히 죽음으로 이끄는 '원인 모를' 병에 시달리게 된다. '슬로우

edge broadens and deepens. This attitude reveals itself in his views on Mr. Park Tae-joon, the Iron King of Pohang, in *Park Tae-joon: a Critical Biography*, and on the North Korean regime in *Big Money and Condoms*.

Lee's supra-ideological approach to understanding people, as influenced by the Cold War system, also led to his interest in the victims of overwhelming, uncontrollable forces. He is especially adept in describing the lives and psychology of those caught under the wheels of history. *Slow Bullet*, in particular, is an excellent example of this.

Slow Bullet, although not widely known, has consistently garnered praise from the readers who have happened to stumble upon. They admire its subject matter, its perfectly plotted story, and its realistic representation of a tragic chapter of modern history.

The title, "Slow Bullet," describes the particular trauma of Vietnam War veterans suffering from the aftereffects of chemical warfare. These victims, suffering from the aftereffects of defoliants inflicted by American troops, find themselves slowly marching to death by way of an unidentified disease. "Slow Bullet" describes the persistent, methodical develop-

불릿, 즉 '느린 탄환'이라는 별명은 이 질병의 끈질긴 전개를 상징하는 것이라 말할 수 있다. 고엽제 환자들은 자신들을 천천히 죽여 가는 보이지 않는 살인자의 손아귀를 느끼며 절망적인 생애를 살아가지 않을 수 없다.

작가 이대환은 역사와 조우하게 된 사람들의 운명에 관심을 가진 작가답게 이 소설 속에서 자신의 고향 호미곶에서 태어난 한 평범한 청년을 베트남으로 보낸다. 젊은 그에게는 숙희라는 이웃 동네에서 자란 애인이 있다. 그는 기름쟁이 생활을 청산하고 목공소를 차려 새 출발을 하겠다는 생활의 설계를 가지고 있다. 이 희망찬 설계 때문에 그는 병장 말년에 장기 근무를 자원하여 베트남 전쟁터로 간다. 입대하기 전 몇 달 동안 '새나라' 택시를 몰았던 그는 운전병이 될 수도 있었지만 박문현 대위의 눈에 띄어 미군 기갑사단으로 차출되어 화학병 교육을 받게 된다. 이것은 그를 그 자신으로서는 절대로 원치 않았을 고엽제 환자로 만들어 버린다.

운명의 장난이라는 점에서는 그의 아내인 숙희도 꼭 같은 경우에 속한다. 이 작품의 결말 부근에서 그녀는 남편을 만나 서로 사랑하며 장래를 약속하던 시절을 회상한다. 아름다운 사랑의 경험은 그녀를 운명적으로 남편의

ment of this disease, the drawn-out, hopeless lives they must lead in the hands of an unknown murderer.

In this novella, Lee sends his main character, an ordinary young man named Ik-su, from his hometown in Cape Homi to Vietnam. Prior to his enlistment, the character's dreams of quitting his job as a mechanic and making a life with his girlfriend, Suk-hui, while establishing his own woodworking shop. In order to fulfill this dream, he volunteers to extend his service and fight in Vietnam. As a former taxi driver, he almost becomes a driver and avoids most of the actual combat and danger. Unfortunately, he loses the opportunity almost immediately when Captain Bak Mun-hyeon intercepts him for chemical warfare training. After training in the American armored forces, he is forced to engage in chemical warfare, resulting in his suffering to the aftereffects of defoliants.

Suk-hui, his wife at this point, also becomes a victim of cruel fate. Towards the end of the novella, she recalls the time when she first fell in love with Ik-su and planned their future together. Their love story is paired it tragically with her husband's present-day agonies. As her husband begins suffering

삶에 연결시킨다. 그러나 남편은 어느 땐가부터 고엽제 후유증에 시달리기 시작한다. 아버지의 병을 물려받은 두 아들을 기르는 그녀는 생활에 쫓기다 못해 해녀가 되기로 결심한다. "내 운명이다." 이 한마디를 심장에 새기고 그녀는 여자로서는 감당하기 어려운 삶을 받아들이는 고행의 시간들을 보낸다.

이 이야기가 독자들의 마음을 더욱 아프게 만드는 것은 영호와 영섭 두 형제마저 아버지의 병을 물려받고 있다는 사실일 것이다. 어느 날 갑자기 하반신 마비가 된 영호, 그리고 사타구니가 짓무르는 이상한 병에 걸려 아버지의 병의 공포를 느끼는 영섭. 아버지의 병이 아들들에게 물려져 그 괴로운 운명을 반복하게 되는 상황은 '슬로우 불릿'이 얼마나 무서운 것인지 실감할 수 있게 한다. 작가는 이 이야기를 아버지 익수의 죽음과 더불어 영호마저 스스로 목숨을 끊는 것으로 끝냈다. 아버지의 병을 대물림한 아들이 스스로 병의 공포에 굴복하기를 거부하도록 한 설정은 개인의 초인적인 의지가 어떻게 역사적인 부조리를 상대할 수 있는가를 시현해 보인 것이라 할 수 있다.

역사라는 것은 인간이 지어내는 것이지만 그럼에도 이 바퀴를 굴리는 인간 집단의 알 수 없는 힘은 그것을 이루

from the prolonged aftereffects of defoliants, she becomes a diver to take care of her family. "This is my fate," she says, and resigns herself to the grueling life of supporting her family alone.

Their story becomes even more tragic when Yeong-ho and Yeong-seop, Ik-su's sons, inherit their father's disease. The two sons' situations mirror their father's painful story: Yeong-ho is paralyzed waist-down overnight and Yeong-seop suffers from symptoms similar to eczema in his groins. Their inherited trauma is the ultimate terror of the "Slow Bullet." The novella ends with Yeong-ho's suicide after his father's death. Yeong-ho's suicide is a final act of resistance against the terror of the disease. It is depicted as an individual's final attempt to combat the absurdity of history.

Although individuals build history, the unpredictable course of their collective actions turns it into a narrative of violence and oppression to the individual. We can call this framing of an individual's struggles *historical fate*. We encounter varying forms of fate throughout our lifetime. When a person dies, perhaps unexpectedly, of local disease on a leisurely tour abroad, we might say that his fate was to die at the insensate hand of nature. When a

는 개체들에 가공할 폭력과 억압이 되곤 한다. 이것을 가리켜 역사적 운명이라 말할 수 있다. 살아서 인간은 여러 형태의 운명에 맞닥뜨릴 수 있다. 만약 한 사람이 아프리카를 즐겁게 여행하다 원인 모를 풍토병에 걸려 갑작스러운 죽음을 맞게 된다면 그것은 그가 자연의 불합리한 힘에 노출된 나머지 죽을 수밖에 없는 운명에 처한 것이라 말할 수 있다. 또 어떤 남자가 한 회합에 나갔다 거기서 자신을 전율케 하는 여자를 만나 평생을 그 여자의 알 수 없는 마력에 끌려다니게 된다면 그것 또한 일종의 운명이라 말할 수 있다. 만약 그녀가 팜므파탈형의 여성이라면 이 남자는 결코 순탄치 않은 인생을 보내다 파멸해 버릴 수도 있다.

인간은 집단으로서는 미스터리한 힘을 가지고 그것을 발동시키지만 개체로서는 그렇게 강한 존재라고 말할 수 없다. 개체로서 그는 그 자신의 삶을 송두리째 바꿔 놓는 힘에 좌우될 수밖에 없는데, 이 가운데 가장 부조리한 형태의 하나가 바로 역사적 운명이다. 한국의 현대사는 세계사를 이루는 어느 민족, 국가의 역사만큼이나 부조리한 힘의 전횡에 시달렸고, 이 역사 전개는 한국인 개개인들의 삶을 파멸로 이끌어 가곤 했다.

man encounters an exceptionally attractive woman, and succumbs completely to her desires, we might call this fate, too. If this woman is a dangerous, consuming, then he might end up being destroyed after riotous, eventful life.

Although human beings are mysteriously powerful as a group, they are not as strong as individuals. Individuals cannot help but to be subject to the collective power that can change their lives at a whim. One of the most absurd forms of this power is historical fate. Modern Korean history has wielded tyrannical power as absurd as that of any other people or country in the world, a historical development that has destroyed countless lives.

Slow Bullet is the story of a family who has to face this destructive fate. The most impressive character in this novella, Yeong-ho, commits suicide. He chooses to fight the disease that slowly kills him with a quick death. Before this choice, he seeks wisdom that will help him control his fate by reading *Zhuangzi* while living in a prayer house. Shortly before his suicide, he tells his father stories from *Zhuangzi*.

Zhuangzi was a philosopher known for a wisdom that superseded the commonsense distinctions of

『슬로우 불릿』은 이 파멸적 운명에 직면한 한 가족의 이야기다. 이 이야기 속에서 가장 인상적인 인물은 그러므로 응당 스스로 목숨을 끊는 영호가 되지 않을 수 없다. 자신을 서서히 죽음으로 몰아갈 질병의 공포에 맞서 스스로 죽음을 선택하는 그는 기도원에 머무르고 『장자』를 읽는 데서 알 수 있듯이 불가항력적인 운명을 다스릴 수 있는 지혜를 갈구하는 인물이다. 그는 죽음의 선택을 앞두고 아버지와 대화를 나누면서 『장자』의 일화들을 이야기한다.

'장주지몽(莊周之夢)'이라는 것으로 잘 알려져 있듯이 장자는 삶과 죽음에 관한 상식과 통념을 뛰어넘는 지혜를 가르쳐 주는 철학자다. 도대체 삶이란 무엇인가. 그것은 과연 어디서 그 실체를 찾을 수 있는가. 꿈속이 실체인가, 꿈 바깥이 실체인가. 우리가 현실이라고 믿는 것이 실체적 현실이 아닐 수 있음을 가르치는 그는 삶이 주는 괴로움을 정관하게 해준다. 작중에서 영호는 아버지에게 장자의 가르침이 담긴 일화들을 이것저것 이야기하는데, 다음은 그 하나다.

"장자가 초나라에 가는 도중에 해골을 만나 말채찍으로

life and death, as famously illustrated in "Zhuangzi's butterfly dream." What is life? What is its substance? Are dreams or the life outside of dreams real life? By teaching us that what we may believe to be real life may not be real, Zhuangzi helps us contemplate on the suffering in our lives. The following is one of the episodes Yeong-ho tells his father.

"When Zhuangzi ran into a skeleton on his way to the country named Chu, he lashed it with his whip and asked, 'How did you become like this? Were you too greedy? Did you have your throat cut in war? Did you commit a wicked crime and kill yourself in order not to dishonor your family? Did you encounter famine? Or, did you live out your fated lifespan?' Then, he slept, using that skeleton as his pillow, and then the skeleton appeared in his dream and said, 'Your words are all about the worries of human lives, and there are no such worries to bother us in the world of death.' So Zhuangzi asked him if he'd like to come back to life if Zhuangzi could petition Yama on his behalf. The skeleton, frowning and with a worried expression, said, angrily, 'Do I seem crazy enough to leave this wonderful world to return to such a hard life in the human world?'

탁 치고 나서 이런 소리를 지껄인 적이 있습니다. 너는 욕망을 탐한 나머지 이 모양이 되었느냐. 전쟁에서 목이 베어졌느냐, 불선한 일을 저질러서 혈육에게 욕을 끼칠까봐 이 모양이 되었느냐, 굶주리는 환난을 당했느냐, 아니면 수명이 그뿐이었느냐. 그러고는 그 해골을 베고 잠을 잤더니 꿈에 해골이 나타나서 너의 말은 모두 인생의 걱정이고 죽음의 세상에는 그 따위 귀찮은 일이 없다고 하더랍니다. 그래서 장자가, 내가 염라대왕을 시켜 그대를 다시 온전한 사람으로 살려줄 테니 환생하겠느냐고 물었더니, 해골이 눈썹을 찌푸리고 수심에 싸여서 하는 말이, 내가 이 좋은 세상을 버리고 미쳤다고 인간의 고생을 다시 하겠느냐고 화를 내더랍니다. 아버지 이게 다.”

죽음에 다다르면 삶의 고통이 없으리라는 장자의 가르침을 옮기는 영호는 이미 자신에게 닥친 운명적인 질병의 고통과 절망을 스스로 손목 핏줄을 절단함으로써 초극하겠다는 의지를 품고 있음을 알 수 있다. 이것을 가리켜 숭고한 죽음의 선택이라고 말할 수 있는 것은 언젠가는 죽을 수밖에 없는 운명을 가진 인간이기에 때로는 삶보다 죽음을 선택하는 것이 그 제한된 수명 속에서 자신의 가

Father, this is all..."

Quoting Zhuangzi's teaching that death eliminates the pain of life, Yeong-ho expresses his will to overcome the pain and despair from his fated disease by terminating his life. We might call this a noble choice. Sometimes choosing death is the best way to maintain one's integrity. We can see a similar example, although in a different context, in Antigone's choice in *Antigone*, where she risks capital punishment in order to bury her brother according to the law of Hades.

Slow Bullet is an invaluable testament to the horrors of the Vietnam War. We still do not know the full details and scope of American chemical warfare in Vietnam. In Lee's novella, Ik-su emphasizes that he dealt with not only the so-called Agent Orange, but also CS powder. Reporters featuring Ik-su's family's suffering show no interest in the whole truth of their plight. But Ik-su suspects that CS powder is one of the "Slow Bullets" that have been plaguing him. Yeong-ho's paraplegia, not a typical symptom of Agent Orange, supports his beliefs. Like Ik-su's and Yeong-ho's unspoken illnesses, the Vietnam

치를 지킬 수 있는 최선의 방법이 되곤 하기 때문이다. 우리는 이 이치를 저 멀리 그리스 비극 『안티고네』 같은 곳에서 일찍이 엿볼 수 있다. 그곳에서 안티고네는 세속의 법을 어기고 죽음의 신인 하데스의 이치를 따라 오빠를 땅에 묻어 스스로 죽음의 형벌을 받는 선택을 감행하고 있다.

한편 『슬로우 불릿』은 일종의 증언문학으로서 중요한 의미와 가치를 지니고 있다. 아직도 미군이 베트남에 살포한 고엽제의 전말은 완전히 밝혀졌다고 말할 수 없다. 작중에서 익수는 자신이 통상적인 고엽제만을 살포한 것이 아니고 '씨에스파우더'라는 약품도 다루었음을 강하게 의식하고 있다.

작중의 방송은 익수의 가족을 고엽제 후유증을 앓고 있는 베트남 참전 용사 가족으로 부각시키지만 '진실'의 총량에는 별 무관심하다. 이에 반해 익수는 이 씨에스파우더가 그 자신을 괴롭히는 '슬로우 불릿'의 정체 가운데 하나일 것이라 의심하고 있다. 아들 영호의 하반신 마비증이 통상적인 고엽제 환자에게서는 나타나지 않는다는 사실은 이러한 의혹에 신빙성을 더해준다. 작가는 이를 통

War continues to have buried truths.

Throughout *Slow Bullet* Lee has an unflinching obligation to the truth. He depicts Ik-su's experience vividly and in detail. The scenes in which Ik-su, the first Korean participant in the chemical warfare, handles CS powder reveals the kind of reality only a writer who thoroughly researches his material can offer. Although rather long, the following shows this point well.

Ik-su was the only person responsible for pouring CS powder out of the sacks and into those containers, like gas canisters, from start to finish. First he created an airtight space using trees and two raincoats. This was done to prevent the poisonous gas from being blown around by the wind. The process was simple. After sticking a funnel into the neck of a container so tall it almost came up to Ik-su's jaw, he poured the powder from the sack. But the poisonous powder, finer than flour, usually did not pour neatly into that tiny, finger-sized hole. Ik-su had to keep poking at the narrow hole with a skewer. He kept shifting this skewer from hand to hand, considering it exercise. But what was maddening was the heat. He always felt that the heat, not the poisonous

해 고엽제 환자들과 베트남 전쟁에 관해서 아직도 더 많은 것들이 파헤쳐져야 함을 알려주고자 한다.

이처럼 '진실'에 관한 의무를 의식한 때문에, 이 소설은 익수의 베트남 참전 경험을 상세하고도 실감나게 재현해 놓고 있다. 한국군 최초로 화학전에 투입된 익수가 씨에스파우더를 다루는 장면들은 자신이 다루고자 하는 소재를 성실하게 조사하는 취재형 작가가 아니고는 선사할 수 없는 실감을 자아낸다. 다소 길지만 이 장면 일부를 여기 옮겨보면 다음과 같다.

포대 속의 씨에스파우더를 가스통 속으로 옮겨 붓는 작업은 처음부터 끝까지 익수 단독으로 처리했다. 맨 먼저 나무를 이용해 판초우의 두 장으로 밀폐공간을 만들었다. 독가스가 바람에 흩날릴 위험을 예방하는 것이었다. 공정은 단순했다. 거의 턱까지 올라오는 가스통의 주둥이에다 깔때기를 꽂아놓고 포대 속의 그놈을 옮겨 붓는다. 그러나 밀가루보다 보드라운 분말 독가스는 손가락을 끼울 만한 구멍 속으로 술술 들어갈 수 없었다. 그가 쇠꼬챙이로 가스통의 협소한 구멍을 쉴 새 없이 쑤셔야 했다. 오른손 왼손 번갈아 쑤시기. 그것은 운동이라 여기면 그만이었

gas, would cause an explosion in that airtight space made from raincoats.

The American instructor taught Ik-su that he had to always wear a gas mask, raincoat, boots, and gloves when handling CS powder. Ik-su started out faithfully following these instructions. But he couldn't last longer than five minutes in all that gear. His body seemed on the verge of boiling. Besides, more containers were waiting by the dozens. He had to dispense with the instructions written in English in heat so intense he thought he would die even if naked. *The military is all about discretion.* He had to become a believer in this dictum. He took off his clothes. He was wearing only an undershirt, shorts and boots. One thing he couldn't take off was the gas mask. He couldn't take it off even if his head would have turned into a boiled pig head on the spot. If he took it off, he would have been suffocated instantly in that airtight space. But he felt strongly tempted whenever he was working with the powder. Luckily he was able to recite a spell that served like an amulet, making him resist that temptation. *I got involved in a war of complete strangers to earn some money. I shouldn't be so crazy as to risk my life pouring poison gas!*

다. 미칠 지경으로 몰아넣는 것은 더위였다. 늘 그랬지만 그의 육감에는 독가스가 아니라 더위가 판초우의의 밀폐 공간을 폭파시킬 것 같았다.

미군 교관은 익수에게 밀폐공간에서 씨에스파우더를 취급할 때는 방독면, 우의, 장화, 장갑 등을 반드시 착용해야 한다고 가르쳤다. 그는 수칙대로 시작했다. 그러나 5분을 견딜 수 없었다. 몸이 삶기는 것 같았다. 더구나 가스통은 10개씩 20개씩 대기하고 있었다. 알몸도 쩌죽을 처지에서 영어의 수칙은 버려서 마땅한 수칙이었다. 군대는 요령이다. 이 진리의 신봉자가 될 수밖에 없었다. 그는 훌훌 벗었다. 윗도리에는 러닝셔츠, 아랫도리에는 팬티와 장화만 남았다. 결코 벗지 못할 또 하나가 있었다. 방독면이었다. 머리가 삶은 돼지머리로 바뀌는 한이 있어도 그것만은 벗을 수가 없었다. 그것을 벗고 덤빈다면 당장 판초우의 안에서 질식할 것이었다. 하지만 작업할 때마다 방독면마저 벗고 싶은 유혹이 강렬했다. 다행히 그는 그것을 물리칠 부적 같은 주문을 욀 수 있었다. 한밑천 잡겠다고 남의 전쟁터에 왔는데 미쳤다고 독가스 옮겨 붓다가 죽어!

빨리 끝내는 것이 상책이란 일념에 매달린 익수가 30분

After about thirty minutes of attentive work, only thinking the sooner he finished, the better, Ik-su would fine that his boots had become slushy inside. Sweat from his entire body was pooling in them. But it didn't seem that big a deal. He could simply take a shower later and drink a lot of water.

As soon as he finished work, Ik-su ran straight to the shower room, like always. Was it because of the sweating? Or, just the heat, generally? No, it was because of his skin. The backs of his hands, his arms, his neck, and his face were swollen and red. It was also very painful. It felt as if innumerable needles were randomly pricking his skin. Standing under the shower, naked, Ik-su waited patiently. He had to wait until the swelling subsided and the redness disappeared. This could take an hour or two. Touching was a taboo. If he happened to scratch or rub his skin, it felt as sore as a burn. Even after his skin became normal, he couldn't use a towel. He couldn't rub it over his skin. He held a towel under his navel and went out. He had to stand naked in well-ventilated shade, sometimes for ten minutes, and other times for twenty. While he was standing like that under a tree, a marvelous moment would arrive, like a promise fulfilled. Suddenly, all the pain

정도 작업에 열중하면 어느덧 발바닥이 질퍽질퍽했다. 온몸의 땀이 장화 속에 모인 것이었다. 하지만 땀은 아무런 문제도 아니었다. 샤워를 해주고 물을 실컷 마셔주면 그만이었다.

작업을 마친 익수는 곧장 샤워실로 달려갔다. 언제나 그랬다. 땀 때문에? 더위 때문에? 아니었다. 피부 때문이었다. 손등, 팔뚝, 목, 얼굴 등이 벌겋게 부어올랐다. 통증도 심했다. 수많은 침들이 한꺼번에 마구 쑤셔대는 것 같았다. 발가벗고 서서 찬물을 맞는 익수의 일은 하염없이 기다리는 것이었다. 한 시간이든 두 시간이든 부기가 가라앉고 벌건 색깔이 스러질 때까지 기다려야 했다. 손은 금물이었다. 긁거나 문지르면 화상처럼 쓰라렸다. 피부가 정상으로 돌아온 다음 차례는 수건을 쓰는 것이 아니었다. 수건으로 닦을 수 없었다. 수건으로 배꼽 밑만 가리고 밖으로 나갔다. 발가벗은 그대로 통풍 좋은 나무 그늘에 들어가서 이십 분이든 삼십 분이든 서 있어야 했다. 나무 그늘 속에 서 있으면 약속처럼 신묘한 순간이 도래했다. 별안간 모든 통증이 사라지고 다시 몸이 싱싱해졌다. 번번이 그랬다. 고생은 길어야 두세 시간이었다.

disappeared and his body felt refreshed. That was always the case. The whole ordeal lasted two to three hours at most.

Scenes like these reveal the authenticity of this novella, guaranteeing its importance as a work that reveals the hidden details of modern Korean history.

People often say that fiction reflects the reality. But I believe that fiction presents the author's reality of the world. If fiction only reflected reality, its work would be passive, ex post facto, even decorative. All the same, representing what has already happened has a very important function in some novels and stories. When higher powers obstruct the truth, fiction can reveal it. This is shown, for example, in *One Man's Bible* by Gao Xingjian, the 2000 Nobel Laureate in literature. Mo Yan, this year's Nobel Laureate in literature, also carried out the same task in his novel *Hong Gao Liang Jiazu*. Gao was exiled abroad and became a French citizen while Mo was a noted pro-government proponent. Nevertheless, both writers performed the same task of revealing historical truths.

Slow Bullet is testimony to the absurd power of authorities that control history and destroy individu-

이러한 장면들이 이 소설의 '진실성'을 보증하는 까닭에 나는 이 소설이 한국 현대사의 다 드러나지 않은 곡절을 드러내는 중요한 작품의 하나가 될 수 있으리라고 생각한다.

흔히들 소설은 세계를 반영하는 것이라고 생각하는 경우가 많다. 그러나 나는 이와 달리 소설이란 세계를 반영한다기보다는 작가 자신이 생각하는 세계상을 제시하는 것이라고 생각한다. 만약 소설이 세계를 다시 보여주는데 그치는 것이라면 소설은 늘 일어난 일에 대해 수동적이고 사후적인 처리를 하는 데 불과할 뿐인, 장식적 작업이 될 수도 있을 것이다.

그러나 동시에 나는 어떤 소설에서는 이미 일어난 일을 다시 보여주는 이 기능이 매우 중요한 역할을 하게 된다고 말하고자 한다. 사태를 장악할 수 있는 위력을 가진 힘에 의해 사태의 '진실'이 가려져 있을 때 소설은 이 '진실'을 드러내는 힘을 발휘한다. 이것을 나는 비교적 근년에도 노벨문학상 수상자인 가오싱 젠의 『나 혼자만의 성경』이라는 작품을 통해 확인할 수 있었다. 지금 내가 이 글을 쓰고 있는 올해의 노벨문학상 수상자는 모옌인데, 이 작가 역시 그의 대표작인 『홍까오량 가족』에서 그와 비슷한

als. The hidden story of the Vietnam War veteran, the story of the victims of both Agent Orange and CS powder, had to be revealed.

Thomas Hardy quotes St. Jerome in the preface of *Tess of the D'Urbervilles*, "If an offence come out of the truth, better is it that the offense come than that the truth be concealed." *Tess of the D'Urbervilles* is the story of a "pure woman" who is victimized by an obstinately prejudicial society, similar to *Slow Bullet*'s story of innocents victimized by a callous world.

Slow Bullet is the record of a family—Ik-su, Suk-hui, Yeong-ho, and Yeong-seop—who were victimized by the absurd developments of modern Korean history. Sincere authors, whether older or contemporary, Western or Korean, cannot avoid their obligation to the truth. Lee worked doggedly in service of this higher goal. His thorough research, tightly woven stories, and controlled, uncompromising problems were all in order to carry out this ultimate obligation to the truth.

일을 해놓고 있다. 한 사람은 망명해서 프랑스 국적을 취득했고, 다른 한 사람은 친정부적인 인사로 알려졌지만, 두 작가는 모두 역사적 '진실'의 존재를 드러내는 역할을 한 것이다.

『슬로우 불릿』은 흔히 오렌지라는 별명으로 불린 고엽제와는 다른 약품까지 다루어야 했던 베트남 참전병의 사연을 중심으로 역사를 주도하는 부조리한 힘이 어떻게 개인을 파멸로 이끌어갔는지 보여준다. 이 사연은 그것이 아직 알려지지 못한 진실이기 때문에 파헤쳐져야 한다.

토마스 하디는 『테스』의 서문에 "진실을 접했을 때 불쾌한 감정이 일어난다면, 그 진실을 감추는 것보다 차라리 불쾌한 감정이 일어나도록 내버려두는 것이 현명하다"라는 성 제롬의 문구를 인용해 놓고 있다. 『테스』는 완고한 편견에 사로잡힌 사회의 위력에 희생되어 가는 "순수한 여인"의 삶을 '기록해 놓은' 작품이었다.

『슬로우 불릿』은 익수, 숙희, 영호, 영섭의 네 식구가 어떻게 부조리한 한국 현대사의 희생양이 되었는지 기록해 놓고 있다. 진실에 대한 의무란 예나 지금이나, 서양에서나 한국에서나, 성실한 작가라면 외면해서는 안 되는 정언 명령이다. 『슬로우 불릿』의 작가는 이 의무를 이행하기 위해 소재를 가려 조사하고, 이를 위한 정밀한 플롯을 짜내고, 말끔한 문장을 창조하는 고단한 활동을 멈추지 않았던 것이라 해야겠다.

번역 전승희 Translated by Jeon Seung-hee

서울대학교와 하버드대학교에서 영문학과 비교문학으로 박사 학위를 받았으며, 현재 하버드대학교 한국학 연구소의 연구원으로 재직하며 아시아 문예 계간지 《ASIA》 편집위원으로 활동 중이다. 현대 한국문학 및 세계문학을 다룬 논문을 다수 발표했으며, 바흐친의 『장편소설과 민중언어』, 제인 오스틴의 『오만과 편견』 등을 공역했다. 1988년 한국여성연구소의 창립과 《여성과 사회》의 창간에 참여했고, 2002년부터 보스턴 지역 피학대 여성을 위한 단체인 '트랜지션하우스' 운영에 참여해 왔다. 2006년 하버드대학교 한국학 연구소에서 '한국 현대사와 기억'을 주제로 한 워크숍을 주관했다.

Jeon Seung-hee is a member of the Editorial Board of ASIA, is a Fellow at the Korea Institute, Harvard University. She received a Ph.D. in English Literature from Seoul National University and a Ph.D. in Comparative Literature from Harvard University. She has presented and published numerous papers on modern Korean and world literature. She is also a co-translator of Mikhail Bakhtin's *Novel and the People's Culture* and Jane Austen's *Pride and Prejudice*. She is a founding member of the Korean Women's Studies Institute and of the biannual Women's Studies' journal *Women and Society* (1988), and she has been working at 'Transition House', the first and oldest shelter for battered women in New England. She organized a workshop entitled "The Politics of Memory in Modern Korea" at the Korea Institute, Harvard University, in 2006. She also served as an advising committee member for the Asia-Africa Literature Festival in 2007 and for the POSCO Asian Literature Forum in 2008.

감수 K. E. 더핀 Edited by K. E. Duffin

시인, 화가, 판화가. 하버드 인문대학원 글쓰기 지도 강사를 역임하고, 현재 프리랜서 에디터, 글쓰기 컨설턴트로 활동하고 있다.

K. E. Duffin is a poet, painter and printmaker. She is currently working as a freelance editor and writing consultant as well. She was a writing tutor for the Graduate School of Arts and Sciences, Harvard University.

바이링궐 에디션 한국 현대 소설 017

슬로우 불릿

2013년 6월 10일 초판 1쇄 인쇄 | 2013년 6월 15일 초판 1쇄 발행

지은이 이대환 | **옮긴이** 전승희 | **펴낸이** 방재석
감수 K. E. 더핀 | **기획** 정은경, 전성태, 이경재
편집 정수인, 이은혜, 이윤정 | **관리** 박신영 | **디자인** 이춘희

펴낸곳 아시아 | **출판등록** 2006년 1월 31일 제319-2006-4호
주소 서울특별시 동작구 흑석동 100-16
전화 02.821.5055 | **팩스** 02.821.5057 | **홈페이지** www.bookasia.org
ISBN 978-89-94006-73-4 (set) | 978-89-94006-75-8 (04810)
값은 뒤표지에 있습니다.

Bi-lingual Edition Modern Korean Literature 017
Slow Bullet

Written by Lee Dae-hwan | **Translated by** Jeon Seung-hee
Published by Asia Publishers | 100-16 Heukseok-dong, Dongjak-gu, Seoul, Korea
Homepage Address www.bookasia.org | **Tel**. (822).821.5055 | **Fax**. (822).821.5057
First published in Korea by Asia Publishers 2013
ISBN 978-89-94006-73-4 (set) | 978-89-94006-75-8 (04810)